The Last Western

The Last Western

CHRISTOPHER LEE BOWEN

ARPress
ILLUMINATING IDEAS
EMPOWERING VOICES

ARPress
45 Dan Road Suite 5
Canton MA 02021
Hotline: 1(888) 821-0229
Fax: 1(508) 545-7580

Ordering Information:

Quantity sales. Special discounts are available on quantity purchases by corporations, associations, and others. For details, contact the publisher at the address above.

Printed in the United States of America.

ISBN-13:   Softcover   979-8-89330-326-1
                eBook   979-8-89330-327-8

Library of Congress Control Number: 2024900550

READER'S COMMENTS

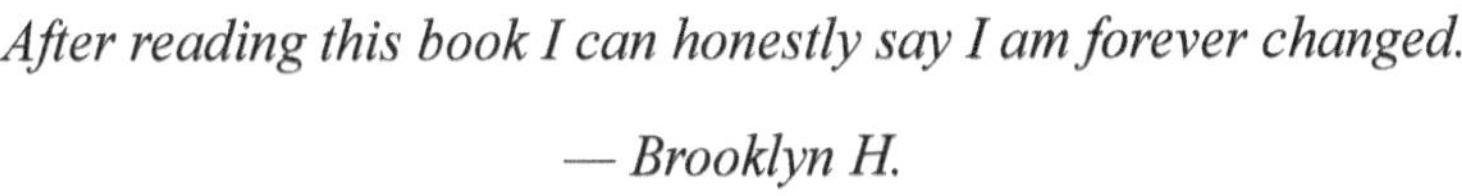

After reading this book I can honestly say I am forever changed.

— Brooklyn H.

Absolutely Great! My daughter adores this book.

— Andrew M.

Great Book! Bowen deserves a big round of applause for this one.

— Wendell J.

Amazing read! Bowen draws out the setting and characters so vividly.

— Yamilie R.

A Baldwin locomotive with six Pullman and five freight cars trailed a black plume of gritty coal smoke across the sere grassland of western Nebraska as it chugged and rattled its way to Del Norte Colorado. The English party, dispirited by the endless monotony of the Great Plains, flocked to the club car to play cards, chat and commiserate. Dressed for tea at a London club, not for the baking heat of June 1882 in midland America, added physical discomfort to their growing misgivings about the trip into the American Wild West. A few sod huts but otherwise no sign of habitation induced a growing sense of leaving civilization behind without a redeeming prospect ahead.

Amanda Egerton, inattentively playing in a foursome of bridge, looked amused by the plush seating, extravagant brass gaslight fixtures and chandelier, lush carpeting and abundant provisions, potable and edible, at the ornate walnut bar of the well-appointed Pullman club car. Velvet seats upholstered in the same garish color her father had once described as 'bordello red' evoked a fond memory of her father, Sir Gavin Egerton, Field Marshall, Baronet, and his biting wit and penchant for mordant comment.

Sir Charles Winthrop, a principal with Imperial Bank of London, sipped whiskey and played poker with Carter Braddock, a New York financier with Peabody-Morgan Bank of New York, a now common international conjunction of capital in chase of resources to exploit. Indistinguishable in appearance, they embodied the industrial age of standardization and interchangeable parts: the same regimental moustache, sleek grey hair, prep-school tie (Harrow/Philips Exeter) black business suit (Savile Row London/Brooks Brothers Boston). Contestants in the ongoing march of English and American capitalism, they met at the Union Club in London, February 1882, to arrange a trip to evaluate prospective copper mines in Colorado.

Lord Basil Pomeroy, a player in the bridge foursome, left his study at Oxford to join the party, reluctantly. Son of the head of Imperial Bank, himself a prospective partner of the bank, and affianced to Sir Charles' daughter Ariadne, Lord Basil felt obliged though uninspired to join the party. Inspiration was not the first characteristic one associated with Lord Basil. Though only twenty-years old, his receding chin, effete manners, and lofty attitude, attributes of declining vigor in the family tree, deprived him of any trace of youthful charm. He was easily unsettled by conditions not arranged to his advantage and convenience.

Sir Charles invited his niece, Amanda, on the trip to chaperone his eighteen-year-old daughter Ariadne while traveling with her fiancé. Not that Lord Basil was a threat to Ariadne's maidenhood, but that she was herself a problem. Expelled from several English finishing schools, she had just recently been discretely removed from Madame Rubique's academy in Geneva, a holding company for stimulating daughters of prominent figures political and financial who needed to be out of the country for a while until a modicum of social self-control was acquired or attendant scandal died down.

Sir Charles, consistent with Darwin's then prevalent evolutionary theories, attributed Ariadne's unruly nature (so incompatible with the Victorian forms to which her mentors tried to mold her) to her French great grandmother, a notable *scandaleuse*, member of the French aristocracy exiled near London in the years of Revolution and Napoleon. A letter from Madame Rubique hinted very discretely, so discretely, that should it fall into the hands of unkind intention it would provide no ground for impugning her character, that Ariadne had a very hot temperament indeed. A three-month visit to her great aunt, la Comptesse d'Aubigny, at age fifteen, instilled very Gallic standards of feminine guile. Her aunt stripped Ariadne nude and evaluated in detail the advantages, function and deployment of every part of her anatomical armory in the battle for money, power, and pleasure. Given her blue eyes, abundant waterfall of chestnut hair, stunning anatomical endowment, and her decolleté dresses cut just short of the limit of social acceptability, Ariadne was ever after an enterprising flirt.

Ariadne Winthrop

"Trump!"

Lord Basil, Ariadne's opponent at bridge, loudly declared victory, a rare event in his courtship. The word 'pyrrhic' crossed Amanda's mind, already persuaded that Ariadne and Lord Basil were entirely unsuited to each other.

"Well done, Basil!"

Exuded Raymond Dumaine, Lord Basil's tutor from Oxford University and bridge partner, invited on the trip to coach Lord Basil for upcoming exams. Sir Charles welcomed anyone who could divert Lord Basil and allow himself to avoid his prospective son-in-law as often as possible without appearance of incivility. Projecting an extraordinary degree of insignificance in manner and person, Raymond was unanimously ignored by the rest of the party.

"I simply must see something vertical, or I shall go mad!!!"

This sudden outburst from Ariadne, presumably exasperated by the loss at bridge or the flat monochromatic landscape of the Great Plains, was in fact inspired by the presence in the club car of a dozen men, a sartorial mélange of bowlers, Stetsons, Brooks Brothers suits, Western frock coats, silk vests, Lucchese cowboy boots, bespoke cordovans, black ribbon bow ties, and shiny silver buckles on hand-tooled leather gun belts. They were headed to a lumber mill in Eureka, a vineyard in Napa, several banks and shipping companies in San Francisco, a ranch in Oregon, a gold brokerage in Sacramento. Varied in appearance, they all shared the vigor of youth. Their frequent glances in her direction assured Ariadne of their considerable, albeit surreptitious, admiration and interest in every move she made.

The men laughed at Ariadne's comment which cheered her up and more than made up for the pyrrhic victory her, by comparison, overdressed and rather effete appearing fiancé had just won at cards. She was more interested in winning at life. Ariadne was excited by the strong, trim, and mostly handsome male fellow travelers in the club car, denizens of a wild land in which social order was maintained by mutually respectful self-defense (their holstered revolvers the means), not enforced by law and instituted authority. Never one to let pass an opportunity to attract and reward male attention, Ariadne set her chin and tossed her long richly auburn hair.

When Ariadne entered the club car all the men immediately rose, removed their hats, nodded and smiled in admiration. Her response was a modest smile, modesty a rarely used ploy in her dramatic repertoire. Masculine aroma of polished leather, Cuban cigars, Jim Beam whisky and bay rum aftershave spread from their end of the club car, their courtesy, admiration and desire to please only slightly tempered their aggressive visual appraisal. Ariadne, used to intimidating the males she encountered in England, now felt a tremor of intimidation herself as their scrutiny suggested no words or gestures of refusal would interrupt their pursuit of pleasure given the opportunity.

Amanda didn't give a damn about bridge, but she was irritated at Ariadne's endemic frivolity and inability to take much of anything seriously. Since her father's funeral two years ago, she lived with her uncle Sir Charles. Amanda and Ariadne shared the tragic early loss of their mothers and got along well enough since neither posed a threat to the goals and expectations of the other. But they were antipodal in temperament. Ariadne willful and impulsive, Amanda thoughtful and reserved, a lovely English girl with green eyes and soft light brown hair widely courted during visits to her father in India. Ariadne looked the quintessential English girl in face, figure, manner and diction, but was inwardly entirely French in feeling, emotion, tastes and outlook. This out of focus combination made all English and most Americans who encountered her uneasy, unable to reconcile apparently shared Anglo heritage of values and outlook with gestures, impulses and expressions entirely Gallic, which were to the Anglo-Americans largely capricious and absurd.

Amanda Egerton

These club car musings and speculations abruptly ended as the train came to a sudden stop. Steel wheels screeched against steel rails as a black mass of buffalo seen outside the club car window moved across the path of the train. All passengers detrained affording Ariadne an opportunity to mingle with the club car male population, evolving into the laughter and banter she especially enjoyed. The men pulled their Colt revolvers to join the hunt. The first shots rang out in a delirium shouts and cat calls. The Sacramento gold broker handed Ariadne his Colt .45 and offered to instruct her on how to aim and fire, necessitating rather intimate proximity. Ariadne hit a buffalo, shrieked with glee augmented by a hug of praise from her tutor to which Lord

Basil found no feasible means of protest. The buffalo panicked and gained speed as they became aware of the first of their number falling under the gunfire.

"Let's get'm stampeding. They'll fall all over each other and trample more than we'll ever shoot."

More laughter and shooting. The gunpowder formed a sooty cloud overhead. Amanda recoiled from the sharp pungent odor as she stepped from the train onto the ground. The men fired as rapidly as they could, Remington rifles, Colt revolvers, like some wild Gettysburg of the Plains. Amanda saw a dozen or more buffalo writhing on the ground as the herd attempted to move around them, couldn't, and began to trample the fallen, tripping more buffalo who in turn were trampled, as the men continued to fire wildly, drunkenly into the herd in a blood fury. Without thinking or knowing what she was doing Amanda began to scream at them: '*Stop, stop this is madness*', pulling at their arms trying to prevent their shooting. They momentarily frowned at her, then smiled: '*Don't you mind pretty lady*' and resumed firing. She finally gave it up and returned to the Pullman car stunned and frightened as if she had looked into the abyss of evil and found it mindless, knowledge of which she would never again be free.

The holocaust ended and the train resumed its journey west, passing the strewn bodies of trampled buffalo. Late in the afternoon, dinner was served in Braddock's private dining car. Tomorrow morning, they would arrive at Del Norte, the English party relieved that the trip was ending but apprehensive as to what could possibly await them in so desolate a place as the American West was turning out to be.

At 11 o'clock in the morning of June 9, 1882, the train pulled into the Del Norte station and Braddock's Pullman and freight cars were detached onto a siding. Fifty cattle in stocks near the station awaited shipment on the eastbound freight train due around two o'clock. The party walked across the station platform past benches where travelers waiting to board the next train east stared amazed at this improbable cast of Dickensian characters. The long wood plank station dock and unprepossessing station house depressed Ariadne, more susceptible than usual to such dips in mood: "*There is absolutely nothing here!*" she exclaimed to Amanda who was looking around enterprisingly for something of interest. Braddock arranged for their trunks and baggage to be removed and taken to the Double-B ranch. He rejoined the party who were standing forlornly on the platform.

"Sorry to desert you like that, but I had to direct delivery of our luggage to the ranch. I realize how depressing all this must look to you, all the better for improving the impression you will have of the ranch. I can at least assure you that there will be a very cold bottle of Dom Perignon to greet you."

Lord Basil, looking dejected, regained composure at the mention of Dom Perignon, smiled wanly, willing to grasp at any promised relief from the endless plains that had occupied his attention moments before. They descended the steps and walked to the carriages. Ranch hands loaded supplies, including crates of wine, brandy and champagne, into a supply wagon. Ariadne, Sir Charles, Amanda, Lord Basil and Braddock got into the most elegantly appointed open carriage. Raymond sat next to the driver, miffed that he had been so relegated, and that dust soiled his immaculate clothes. He tugged angrily at his cuffs as the driver slapped the two mares into action. *Vamanos!*

In front of the general store, Leah Featherstone was helping her father load dry goods into a wagon sent from one of the large ranches. She noticed the elegant party ride by. Braddock, assuming a democratic smile, waved and said *"Hello! "* Leah and her father waved back: *"Welcome to Bridger!"*, unable to think of anything more heartening to say to the stunned tired faces of the other members of the party.

Leah Featherstone

Sir Charles produced a sliver of a smile, and immediately turned to remark something to Sir Basil to his right. Only Amanda looked up, smiled and waved at Leah, a lithe very attractive girl with long lustrous black hair and a shy friendly smile wearing a colorful beaded deerskin Indian dress. Leah noticed Amanda was looking at her, blushed, then turned modestly back to loading business. Ariadne just sulked.

Del Norte served as a railhead from which to ship cattle to Chicago stockyards. One wide dirt road ran from the train station straight through town past a saloon, hotel, blacksmith, general store and post office, law office, doctor's office, courthouse, jail, and two churches, one Baptist and one Episcopal, the latter built three years before to serve the wealthy summer vacationers from back east. Women shoppers stepped onto the verandah of the general store to observe the Braddock party. A few cowboys, squinting into the Sun from under their wide

Stetsons, left the saloon to stare at the women, dressed more for a stroll in Hyde Park than for the wilds of Colorado. A drunken Indian sat on the ground sleeping outside the saloon, his head nodding forward, oblivious of the glory passing before him. Long- johns, nightshirts, pants, bloomers, dresses fluttered in the gentle breeze on clothes lines beside rudimentary wood shacks scattered around the town perimeter. The bare, unadorned monotony of the town deepened Ariadne's despond plunged her into a silence totally in contrast to the pert and provoking conversation typical of her during the trip west.

Wealthy easterners lived out of town on their ranches that provided centers for entertainment and visits between their owners. Del Norte was merely a supply and transportation hub seldom otherwise visited, except for Sunday services at the Episcopal Church. Father Allen Montescue lived at the parsonage, the only respectable residence in town. Desperate for company, he traveled obsessively to the ranches for dinners and social occasions, staying overnight if he could wangle invitations.

Twelve miles due north of Del Norte was an Indian reservation of some nine thousand Sioux, not that anyone was interested enough to make an accurate census of its population. A number of Indians and half breeds scrounged whisky and an existence in town. The Indian Agent, Philip Cadwallader, rented a room at the local hotel, as did Sheriff Robert Westmoreland. Philip attempted to protect Indian interests and ensure fair treatment and compliance with treaty provisions. The Sheriff maintained law and order, allowing for the noisy exuberance of itinerant cowboys and the whisky and other diversions available at the saloon. Most of his 'clients' were drunk and disorderly patrons of the saloon. He put them in a cell but left it unlocked so they could leave when sobered up. Some regularly tried to get arrested, considering the jail as a warm flop house with free breakfast courtesy of town taxpayers, of greater comfort than alternatives available under conditions of liberty.

At Fort Polk, seven miles east of Del Norte, a cavalry troop of one hundred thirty bluecoats discouraged Indian outbreaks and protected from highwaymen wagon trains of settlers headed west to Utah, Oregon, and California. The fort, home to a large group of idle males desperate for diversion. was an economic boon to Del Norte, whisky, sex, cards and merchandise finding a reliable, profitable and inexhaustible market. Only the commander of the Fort, Colonel Ambrose Drake, was invited to enjoy the hospitality of neighboring ranch owners. The other officer and men left to find whatever recreation was obtainable at the Bridger saloon, tended by its owner and three barmaids, available for a price, rising or falling according to their evaluation of the looks and gentility of the petitioner. A few squaws, unencumbered by discriminatory criteria, were also available at substantially lower rates.

The Double-B ranch was five miles from Del Norte. Easterners owned most of the land within twenty miles. Hired cowboys managed the ranches year-round visited by their owners only from late spring to early fall, depending on their business commitments back east. The ranch managers, mostly veterans of the Confederacy and many cattle drivers, considered their job lucrative but unmanly, especially dealing with rich eastern dudes and their hobby ranches. A motley crew of cowboys made up the ranch staff yearlong--Mexican, Indian, Negro, Drifter, Outlaw--whoever was willing to work and maintain a modest level of responsible conduct. Economic viability is not a primary concern, but the ranches were run to pay for themselves so far as possible. Ranch houses were elaborate, even fanciful buildings lavishly furnished and landscaped.

The party reached the Double-B ranch about noon. The dusty trip on a long dirt road through barren landscape augured ill so far as the English were concerned, but they brightened immediately as they approached the ranch house. A large rambling two-story stucco and timber residence with slate roof and leaded glass windows appeared mirage-like, a horizontal version of a 17th Century Stratford town house. Abundant plantings of cottonwood and aspen trees, the lovely, shaded lawn and flower beds bordering the house, created an oasis particularly welcome, suggesting the cherished English country houses they had left behind. Braddock of course had long experience of the impression his ranch made on guests after the comparative desolation of the ride from town.

Raymond descended from the driver seat to confront face to face a stocky Mexican about to remove luggage from the supply wagon.

Had he been in deepest Borneo such a contrast between two human specimens could not have been more striking. Once Ariadne and the rest of the English party entered the house, they sighed with collective relief and some admiration, the move to rooms made with considerable anticipation. No sense of the prairie or the west entered the house. One might have been in New York or London. Oriental rugs, Victorian and Sheraton furniture, a Steinway grand piano, formal mantelpieces for fireplaces in the parlor, dining room, hall and upstairs bedrooms. The wide entry was tiled in checkerboard black and white marble. The staircase was carved with walnut, elegantly covered with deep pile red carpet.

The house is divided into two large wings. Upstairs, women were assigned rooms in the west wing, gentlemen in the east wing. Each bedroom was a suite with separate sitting room, Queen Anne furnishings, bedroom with canopy bed, bathrooms with the latest water closet and bath. Sitting rooms had beautiful picture windows, curtains in discreet patterns to soften the light. Lush oriental rugs covered the oak floors, providing an atmosphere of rich quietude that was particularly reassuring.

"You all need to recover and settle in. My staff will help you in every way, and if you need anything, at any time just ring. We can meet for champagne and lunch in an hour."

Braddock's solicitude, as if coddling stranded children, might have irritated under familiar circumstances, but they were at sea in a very strange and alien environment and welcomed his words. They were shown to their rooms by what seemed to be a ubiquitous supply of Mexican maids who appeared and disappeared almost telepathically.

"What a strange place. This house is magnificent but how are we going to survive for the next three months in this desert?"

Ariadne is characteristically ambivalent. Amanda admitted that the town was spare compared to New York, but Braddock's ranch house was respectably furnished and nicely landscaped. She particularly liked the large trees that framed the blue sky visible from the large bay window of their bedroom.

"There are horses Ariadne, and you can at least ride yourself to exhaustion to relieve the boredom. I understand there will be a party day after tomorrow so we shall meet more people and I am sure someone of interest will turn up."

They returned downstairs. Lunch served in the large dining room, a rectangular walnut table with white linen, silverware, china, crystal, unlit candles in a large candelabra and a crystal chandelier hung impressively over an enormous silver bowl of fresh cut flowers. Each held a glass of champagne served by the Mexican butler on a large silver platter, two bottles of Dom Perignon rested on a serving cart near the entrance to the dining room. Braddock lifted his glass.

"To you lovely ladies whose beauty is greater than all the tribute we can pay to it."

Or something like that. However tired the sentiment might have sounded under more familiar circumstances (certain to provoke a mocking aside from Ariadne), on this occasion in this desolate place, serving as a reassertion of civilized forms and gracious manners, his words were received with such welcoming approval that even Ariadne had a small tear in her left eye. She smiled forcefully at Braddock as if to underscore and capitalize her approval. Following lunch, they drank more champagne and its unfailing magical effect relaxed and enlivened the guests, who an hour before might have more easily dissolved in tears as engage in sparkling repartee. The more Ariadne drank, and she did not intend to limit herself apparently, the livelier she became.

"My dear Mr. Braddock, you have brought us to this wilderness for your own dark purposes, but surely you have planned some suitable entertainment for us short of Indian rain dances in leather loincloths by the light of the Moon."

"Miss Ariadne, we will introduce all of you to our little colony the day after tomorrow. I think you will have an entirely different impression of them than you have had of our west so far. Of course, the real question is why are we out here at all? I'm afraid I have to blame it all on Darwin."

Raymond, systematically ignored, ever susceptible to academic posturing, perked up at the evolutionary allusion, took his chance to insert himself into the general conversation. *"My word, how so Braddock?"* Having mellowed in mood after champagne, ample Chablis, and a succulent pheasant main course with fresh fruit, chocolate mousse, Braddock and company were prepared to overlook this impertinent inquiry by a person no one but Lord Basil had deigned to engage with since the train left New York. Braddock ignored Raymond and addressed himself to Sir Charles.

"Quite simply, Sir Charles. Since he launched his 'survival of the fit' theory, everyone here has been complaining how soft we have become in our New York banks, clubs, and mansions. Ruggedness is the new byword, and so some idiot, probably Teddy Roosevelt, a noted health freak, bought a ranch out here and hundreds more have followed him into the wilderness. I find the whole thing preposterous, but for business reasons I can hardly absent myself from their summer frolic and expect to do business with them the rest of the year. So, fitness is their program I subscribe to publicly, but have no intention to let it spoil my domestic enjoyments. May I offer anyone more Champagne?"

Ariadne, already well lubricated, advanced her glass.

"Thank you, Mr. Braddock. If I weren't already spoken for I should make advances to you as by far the most sensible man I have ever met."

Braddock smiled in her direction.

"And that is the greatest compliment I have ever received."

The party laughed in good spirits at this remark, a solidarity of outlook taking positive shape.

"I hear that you and Amanda are great Amazons and I want especially to place at your disposal two of my finest Arabians. The riding hereabouts is quite good. Even the scenery is of interest once you get used to the reduced range of variation in color, altitude and species. But the horse is the main thing for the rider, and I can guarantee you will have a prime example."

Braddock smiled at Amanda and Ariadne, thereby improving their dispositions and inspiring a trace of optimism. A party, new faces, good horses, a well provided table, one could do worse in the godforsaken wilds of the American West. Shortly after, the men, with the exception of Raymond, who dourly and entirely unnoticed, returned to his room, went into the library for cigars, while Amanda and Ariadne went outside onto the veranda. Sir Charles and Lord Basil entered the library. Bookshelves of leather-bound books, deep leather sofas and easy chairs, large oil lamps, gave the room a clubby feel that put them immediately at ease. Had they looked out the lozenge-paned leaded windows and seen St. Paul's cathedral they would not have been surprised.

"Sir Charles, we will stay here a few days to recoup from the trip, but I would like to take you and Lord Basil to the prospective mine site and meet our field engineers. They have been surveying the area and will report on their findings."

"Excellent idea. Both Lord Basil and I need to get first-hand knowledge of operations here. If we can return with ore samples and other evidence of sound prospects, all the better."

He sipped his brandy, the quality of which added another pleasant surprise to the series begun with champagne before lunch. Lord Basil assumed an optimistic look and tone to match his prospective father-in-law, despite inner misgivings about where and under what circumstances the trip would take place. An extended period in the saddle eating dust and broiling in the sun would hardly be compensated by whatever 'first-hand knowledge' Sir Charles anticipated. Assuming a tone of casual inquiry he turned to Braddock.

"Where are the mining operations, Braddock?"

"Thirty miles west, about a day and a half on horseback. We'll take enough servants and provision to keep things as agreeable as possible. The entire trip should take no more than ten days."

As if reading Lord Basil's concern, he added:

"It will be roughing it of a sort, but I have no intention of giving up whatever degree of comfort I can provide."

Lord Basil smiled appreciatively at such civilized sentiments. Sir Charles, having restored his spirits, began to feel rather adventurous, looked with annoyance at Lord Basil's poorly concealed concern about even a modicum of roughing-it discomfort in the great outdoors.

"A little camp life will do us good, Braddock. Maybe your friends are right about our getting too soft. I for one look forward to the trip."

He took another sip of brandy, drew on his cigar and blew a plume of smoke toward Lord Basil's left ear, where it lingered contemptuously for more than a minute.

James Westmoreland, in spite of the Stetson, cowboy boots, and Sheriff's star, had an urbane gentlemanly reticence that no one who knew him mistook for weakness. He was tall, lean, large-boned, a craggy Scotch-Irish face that would be described as handsome in a rugged outdoors way. His sandy hair and clear blue eyes gave him a grace of youth that combined with the strong lines of his face, the traces of suffering overcome, the general sympathy for people in his look, to engage immediate liking and confidence. He spoke in a low, soft voice with a Virginia accent capable when needed of tightening without a rise in volume to show the force and determination that under lay his character.

Westmoreland had served in the Confederate cavalry, fought in several major campaigns and many skirmishes, and lost his wife and daughter to marauders in Mississippi late in the war, wife raped and murdered, daughter shot and left for dead. Both were buried by negroes on his plantation, who told him what happened when he returned home from the war. He never recovered. It wasn't revenge, it wasn't as simple as hatred. It was an imbalance, an account that remained to be settled, no longer personal, or at least not predominantly personal. Something carried over that had to be resolved before life could begin again. That something was hard to define, but it was still important to Westmoreland seventeen years after the end of the war. For Westmoreland the war had not ended. He lost his plantation to carpetbaggers and came north in 1872 with a cattle drive from Texas, hired on as a ranch manager and was elected Sheriff in 1878. Which explains why he was seated at his desk in the Sheriff's office in Del Norte, Colorado, when Philip Cadwallader came through the front door.

Philip looked upset. In someone so boyishly youthful it looked charming. He was from a prominent Philadelphia Quaker family, rich in banking despite their religious doubts about the moral value of money. Philip was also tall, lean and handsome in a boyish version, with clear grey-blue eyes and pink complexion that disarmed anyone who dealt with him. He was earnest, moral, truthful, and dedicated. For most people that was unfortunate because his virtues were directed toward benefiting the Indians, and no one in Del Notre but Philip gave a damn about Indians. He had joined the Indian Bureau as an Indian Agent in 1880, after graduating from Haverford College. His parents smiled desperate smiles as he explained his vocation to save and protect the downtrodden Sioux. Though in theory supportive of such moral commitment, in practice they doubted it would come to any good. Long experience in the snake pits of commercial banking tempered the original 'God will provide' idealism if not delusion of Quaker belief. Couldn't he just work at the bank, donate money to Indian relief funds, and perhaps spend a few weeks in Summer vacation on onsite assistance? Philip insisted, and they agreed that as the youngest son he was not needed immediately to maintain family succession at the bank. He could try the job as Indian Agent for two years. Then the entire family would reassess the situation. That reassessment would take place in the Fall when he returned to Philadelphia for vacation.

Philip had come to inform Westmoreland that gun runners had delivered rifles to the Sioux reservation. Indians were poor, and sympathetic groups, mainly churches in the East, had raised money to help them. Some of that money was directed toward their practical need for weapons to defend themselves.

Philip and Westmoreland were close without being in any way similar. Westmoreland liked Philip for his idealism. He had long since stopped hating the Indians, without feeling any injustice had been done them. Westmoreland was pragmatic, and it was obvious that

White settlement of the west was inevitable. He was aware, however, that the US Army was conducting silent war against the tribes contrary to recent Federal laws and treaties. He and Philip believed in principles of honor and fairness, which in Westmoreland's case overrode law and official directives. After Little Big Horn nearly every career Army officer was committed to extermination. Gradually, Westmoreland came to the conclusion that some balance of power was needed to prevent this. He also came to see the Indians in his own light as a Confederate soldier--gallant fighters in a lost cause.

He had been riding the county roads late at night for several weeks in an attempt to intercept gun traders. Two nights before he encountered a wagon and checked the load. He found fifty obsolete rifles and ammunition. He looked at the driver and trader for a long minute, then remounted and turned back to town. His men had used similar rifles in the war. They had lower muzzle velocity than the new Remingtons of the Union Army, but the Rebels aimed better and had stronger nerves which helped compensate for inferior fire power. The Indians couldn't do any offensive damage with the guns, but they might at least defend themselves. It wasn't a favor, it wasn't even an act of charity, it was simple fairness. If he accused them of receiving rifles, he couldn't protect them from charges of treaty violation, and they would become even more vulnerable.

Philip flung himself into an armchair near the door. Westmoreland nodded sympathetically and pushed a bottle of water toward him. Two glasses were always next to the bottle. Philip poured a glassful.

"I wouldn't worry about the Indians having guns. I'd worry about them not having guns. No amount of treaty compliance will protect them from Army attacks if Colonel Drake decides to move against them."

Westmoreland frowned, then smiled and resumed on a lighter note.

"So, have you heard from home lately? Do your parents still think you are as crazy as the rest of us do?"

Philip relaxed as they resumed their year-long conversation about life, justice, the fate of the underdog, their different opinions about the Civil War, the importance or folly of nonviolence. Philip never carried a pistol and only carried a rifle when going into the backcountry to protect his horse from rattlesnakes and wolves. He was, however, oddly contradictory it might seem, a dead shot. On a few occasions, Westmoreland would drag him out back to shoot skeets, just to keep in practice. *"Justice needs a gun Phil, especially where the arm of the law cannot reach."* Coming from the Sheriff, those were meaningful words.

Fort Polk, the prototype of much later grade-B western movie sets, consisted of a pine stockade, headquarters building and Commandant residence, a flagpole with stars and stripes and a blue cavalry troop flag dancing gaily in the light breeze, wooden barracks for the troop, a mess hall with a wisp of smoke coming out of the kitchen chimney, haul wagons parked near the entry gate, and latrine, shower stalls and stables outside the walls. No litter, nothing out of place. Despite the crude materials and structures, the fort had a pervasive look of immaculate order, unlike any other in the west. One person accounted for that.

Colonel Ambrose Drake stepped onto the porch of his headquarters building and started down the steps. Private Hans Becker held the reins of Drake's horse, eyed the Colonel carefully. The entire company, standing at ease in formation, also eyed the Colonel. One got to know how to read the signs of mood and temperament of the man who, to the extent life, death, and mainly pay could be held in one man's hands under the anarchic conditions of the western frontier, more or less determined their survival.

Drake was not happy, and he usually shared his unhappiness as widely and as soon as possible. His request for transfer had again been denied. Another year in this godforsaken fort in store. As he squinted to adjust to the bright sunlight of mid-morning, he looked with generic malice at the blur of bluecoats standing before him. Lieutenant Jeffrey Chapin, West Point 1881, called the company to attention.

"Company, ten-hut!!"

Drake moved down the line. Sergeant Murphy winked at Chapin, not amusedly but as a signal that things could get ugly. The troop, having repaired the states of dishevelment not totally eradicable on a Sunday following the Saturday night binge, stared straight ahead as Drake passed.

Drake was impressive, no doubt about it. At six feet two inches, one-hundred ninety pounds, he was lean, mean, haggard, his deep-set green eyes glinting with pain, anger and the relentless darkness of an experienced killer. The morphine at least began to take effect, relaxing the tension in his jaw and shoulders. Although physically almost awe inspiring, like some lion king scarred and torn by many battles but ever victorious and unchallengeable, his dress was immaculate. Not always. During the war he hardly kept buttons on his tunic. Serving in six major campaigns and then as head of marauders late in the war, he had been wounded three times, the last at Chattanooga in 1863. For two months he lay shot full of morphine, the wonder drug of the Civil War, one of more than two-hundred thousand addicts who survived field hospitals. Doctors gave him little chance to recover, but somehow, he willed himself back to health. He was fit enough to return to duty in 1864. General Grant, his friend in Indiana before the war, put him in charge of marauders figuring he could do no harm and some good. He did a lot of both, harm to the Confederates and good for himself. At the end of 1864 he was promoted to temporary rank of Brigadier General in charge of all special units operating in the South. Though by then addicted to morphine and equally dependent (as was Grant) on alcohol, he could function as coldly and effectively under their influence as he ever had without.

An almost maniacal look of frozen determination made his men more afraid of him than the enemy, driving themselves to actions they later found shocking, in some cases so undermining that they never again could adjust to civilian life. Whatever sense of cause or purpose they had begun the war with was now a faded memory during the brutal slaughter of Confederate women and children in a campaign of civilian terror to break the South's will to resist. Many remained in the Army as a refuge from the acts that haunted them. So long as they were subject to the authority that originally sanctioned those acts, their conscience could be assuaged by whisky and a sense of placing responsibility for their actions in other hands.

Drake didn't need assuaging. He accepted responsibility and gave orders. He was a fighter, and nobody even thought of challenging him. After the war he was granted a regular commission as Major and offered a post in Washington. He worked hard for General Grant's election in 1868 and was rewarded by promotion to Lieutenant Colonel. In the course of Grant's first term Drake served as Congressional liaison and often visited the White House, drinking and playing cards well into the early hours. Grant signed his commission as full Colonel in 1870. In 1876, Drake was about to be promoted Brigadier General and assigned to California, when an unfortunate dustup at a party hosted by Senator Young cast fatal doubts on the promotion and appointment. As chairman of the Senate committee that oversaw the Army Department, Young held the fate of service promotion and assignment and nothing Grant could do would change his mind about Drake.

Some said it was Drake's rumored morphine addiction, others that it was Drake's unusually aggressive (and successful) attitude toward others' wives that accounted for the Senator's implacable hatred. The real reason was Drake's success with the Senator's tipsy nineteen-year-old daughter in an upstairs bedroom during a party. The depth of the Senator's aggravation could be gauged by the fact that he made sure Drake was assigned to the west in a post as remote as possible.

For six years, Drake had been drifting from fort to fort fighting Indians with more success than he had fighting the bureaucracy in Washington. Young had by now retired from the Senate and other players were in charge, but the record stood against Drake's chances for rehabilitation, despite strong field reports of his valor in the ongoing Indian wars. Valor might be a rather strong word to use. The Indians were hardly a worthy enemy equal in equipment and resources, but Drake approached them with a casual ruthlessness few could imitate. Some residual sense of human decency held back even the most rabid Indian fighters, leaving to the unconscionable the task of outright extermination.

After the Civil War, Drake took on a personal campaign that seemed incongruous to those who had seen his soiled button-less tattered uniform, or what passed for one, during campaigns. He became immaculate, tailored, fanatical, almost a dandy about the quality, fit, and condition of his uniform. Such conduct in anyone else might have inspired satirical comment. But the cold green of his eyes, the creased coarse oddly handsome planes of his face, the drooping salt and pepper moustache under which surprisingly large white teeth showed when he smiled at receptions and embassy events, made any levity or even comment about his appearance totally unlikely and definitely unwise.

Even in the west on the campaign trail, he regularly changed uniform. On formal occasions in Washington, he stood out with particular brilliance for his lean, well-tailored appearance. Army command in Washington automatically sent embassy invitations to his desk, figuring his formidable looks and spotless appearance would impress whatever foreign military attaché he happened to encounter.

At the fort he was surprisingly indulgent to the men, perhaps realizing that spruce dress was irrelevant, a personal preference. He was not indulgent about fighting qualities or training, sponsoring boxing and wrestling matches and intensive physical fitness, and driving the men out at all hours of the night for what were loosely called maneuvers. His own tireless participation, deadly accuracy of fire with rifle or pistol, matchless horsemanship, left no one grumbling openly. A stunned admiration seemed to bind the men to him, although he hardly cared if they lived died. Not that he was indifferent to their requirements. He fought for and got prompt salary payments, promotion, supplies, arms, ammunition, horses, mules. He was a scourge of the Quartermaster Corps. But he did this as if providing for the maximum efficiency of a machine which he expected to use to its limits.

He was no moralist. Whisky? A necessity which he tolerated and even encouraged, provided it didn't interfere with duty. During the war the Army ran on whisky and only a fool would suppose that an addiction to the sauce disqualified a man from distinguishing himself in battle. After all, Grant was a drunk. Drake was seldom without a flask and had gained more battle experience and honors than any soldier he now led. Most had only fought Indians, which Drake thought of as shooting ducks in a barrel, something he unfortunately did not think was particularly reprehensible.

Women? Drake to all outward appearances cared not at all about women on any personal level. He was not a misogynist, he was not a skirt chaser. His rugged handsome appearance and atmosphere of danger scared some, fascinated others, but attracted all. There were rumors that he had been married, lost his wife tragically, and never recovered from his last great love. Such rumors attend strong, solitary figures. One look at Drake cast doubt on such romantic notions, but who could say that far in his past such an event didn't take place, shaping his life and then deforming it.

He had a Mexican cook, broad-faced Conchita, about as fat as humanly possible, and her husband Jose, who did heavy chores and took care of Drake's horses. Estrellita, a seventeen-year-old Mexican girl served as a 'general maid'. She was beautiful, with long black hair, honey-brown complexion, flashing black eyes. She wore a different multicolored dress with swing skirts, had silver and turquoise jewelry, and wore red sandals. Every Sunday Drake would take her riding. Evenings the troop heard a piano, music they didn't recognize. Nobody ever mentioned Estrellita to his face.

Estrellita

Drake had one professional goal. To be as perfect as possible in the use of the Remington rifle, the Colt .45, and the Bowie knife. He had Bowie knives custom made in Massachusetts to his specified weight of 2.15 pounds. The blade and handle were of his own design, and he ordered nearly twenty knives a year as prizes for troopers who demonstrated proficiency in knife throwing. He devised a four by seven feet target of pine board two-inches thick, covered with a cotton duck pad on which the outline of a human figure was painted in black. The board was mounted on wheels. Behind were braces which two men held to roll the board in random directions.

Drake would take a Bowie knife, turn his back to the target, while men rolled the board around thirty to forty yards away. He would turn and throw the knife with unvarying accuracy from any angle. The men moving the board looked with understandable alarm at the blades crashing through the cotton stuffing and thick wood. Knives were retrieved by Jose, who beamed admiration as he pulled them from the board, a physically demanding effort even for his three-hundred-pound frame. Drake ordered his men to practice knife throwing and hand to hand combat with wooden knives that often led to injuries.

Drake also practiced skeet shooting with rifle and revolver. A soldier would throw a skeet behind Drake's back, call '*UP*', and Drake would turn, sight and fire wherever the target happened to be. He never missed. Such exercises were more effective than speeches in imposing awe and obedience among the troops. The men of the fort became almost cultist in their obsession with Drake, the supreme fighter. In their own exercises they vied for recognition. Drake supported boxing and wrestling matches and awarded liberal leave and exemption from kitchen and latrine duty for the winners. A core of exceptionally skilled fighters formed unofficially at the center of a dedicated troop. Unlike most other forts in the West, desertion was rare, usually more a matter of driving off unsuitable recruits than having to retain those he already had. This record amazed higher ranks in Washington. Amazing people seemed to be Drake's principal characteristic, all the more successful for his not caring a damn how he impressed others or what they might think.

Drake saluted Private Hans Decker, took the reins and mounted in a brisk graceful swing, snapping into the right stirrup like clockwork. His horses were always the most expensive, best groomed, and best saddled. An undivided will seemed to join him and his mount, every move like a Centaur with no sense of a rider on a horse. He was going to the Double-B reception for the English newcomers, with some curiosity. Braddock had sent a confidential note about some business matters he wanted to discuss, and Drake felt it was important to keep this potentially politically advantageous connection well oiled. He clicked his tongue and Starlett, his black Arabian, sparked into a trot, Drake saluting the colors as he rode out the gate. The troop continued to look after him for nearly a minute after he had turned and disappeared from view.

The reception at Double-B ranch took place in a large pavilion built in a cottonwood grove some fifty yards from the main house. Braddock had anticipated the need for a social center and the scattered neighbors had come to think of the pavilion as a community center, engaging it for their own entertainments, so that it was in frequent use. It was covered by an oiled canvas roof in case of rain. Pine flooring provided a large dance area and gathering place pleasantly open to air and light, enclosed by awnings in case of high wind or inclement weather. Refreshment tables and barbeque located just outside the pavilion, also under canvas. Tables set with food and drink at the north end of the pavilion and bandstand at the south end. Cowboys, Mexican ranch hands and domestic staff with a mix of fiddles, guitars, banjos, flutes, buckskin drums and mariachis, and an upright piano played waltzes, polkas, square dances and Steven Foster songs. The Mexicans, completely transformed from their daily appearance, wore colorful shirts, wide-brimmed hats, silver belt buckles and silver tipped boots.

Amanda thought it the drollest collection of musicians she had ever seen but admired their vigor and virtuosity. Ariadne looked impatient and annoyed. She was skeptical that the guests who were beginning to arrive, would turn out to be any relief from the monotony of the prairie. She was already counting the days remaining before their return to England.

Colonel Drake rode into the yard as a cluster of guests arrived. He looked around without interest. Mrs. Lefranc, wife of the French banker from New York, came up to Drake and led him to Amanda and Ariadne. *'Vous devez faire la connaisance de nos amies anglaises. Et puis, j'ai besoin de votre aide'. 'A votre service, madame'*, he replied with an obliging smile. Among the many mysteries surrounding Drake was determining when exactly he might have learned French, in addition to Spanish, which he also spoke fluently. She introduced him to Amanda and Ariadne. Drake shook Ariadne out of her querulous mood by remarking that she resembled Venus in Botticelli's painting in Florence, something about which she had no certain knowledge to judge the perspicacity of his remark, but recognizing a compliment derived from a refined observation of an universally esteemed work of art, she smiled and bowed ever so slightly showing the ample contours of her remarkable bust as if to confirm the analogy. Mrs. Lefranc then led Drake away, speaking rapidly and in a low voice, as he looked back at Ariadne and smiled.

Lord Basil formed the nucleus of a group of women appropriately impressed with his title. The unfailing smiles and admiration in which he basked relieved his growing anxiety over the upcoming trip. Most of the women were trim, well-endowed and good looking, a source of admiration not often experienced in England.

Brandon Evans, the Double-B ranch manager, lingered near a cluster of cottonwoods smoking a cheroot. He had run the ranch for three years, having signed on as a ranch hand five years ago. Six feet two inches, strapping, blue-eyed, chestnut hair, hard handed, Brandon was raised on a family plantation in South Carolina including a patrician social formation and an adequate but unambitious education at a prep school in Charleston. Loss of family property and wealth to carpetbaggers after the war forced him to drift west, join cattle drives in Texas and assume an entirely new way of life from the white columns and crowded stables of his patrimony. He looked at Amanda and Ariadne with gentlemanly curiosity as to why they were here.

Brandon Evans

Braddock invited him to a large social gathering perhaps in grudging recognition of Brandon's better times and upbringing superior to his present circumstances. Maybe Braddock saw in him a fellow spirit, a younger version of himself, perhaps unconsciously a surrogate son. He and Brandon got along without any seeming personal liking, strictly business. Brandon kept the men in line and at work, the herd in order, and the bottom line black. He asked for a raise a year ago, promptly given.

The band began playing a waltz, which attracted a number of couples to the dance floor. James Westmoreland, who had been talking with Philip Cadwallader, looked for Amber Bradshaw, the mayor's daughter, saw her near the buffet, and walked over. He was eternally amazed that such a gelatinous, overweight unprincipled conniver as Owen Bradshaw could have produced such a lovely daughter. Her blush and sparkling blue eyes never failed to ignite paternal feeling and undoubtedly other feelings he wasn't yet prepared to acknowledge to himself. In any case, gossip linked them by the most tenuous thread, since he never visited her or saw her apart from the very public social occasions to which everyone was invited.

"Care to dance Amber."

She blushed and said she would.

"You surprised me, Mr. Westmoreland."

"That in itself is a compliment. That at my age that I could surprise anyone makes up for being almost unsurprisable myself, except for when I see your beautiful eyes."

The sight of an elegant, beautiful girl in a lovely ball dress simply drew out the Southern gallantry from somewhere in his careworn past. Left on his own, Philip walked over to Amanda.

"Excuse me, I'm Philip Cadwallader, Indian Agent hereabouts. We are delighted to welcome you to the notorious American West, an intimidating experience at first. May I have the pleasure of this dance?"

His smooth but somewhat archaic formality pleased Amanda, as though some rigor in manners was a reassuring antidote to her overall impression of informality, lack of form, even a disposition to violence in the country and people so far.

"I'd be delighted. My name is Amanda Egerton. And the west is quite intimidating. But I have had some practice dealing with exotic places, having lived in India and Egypt. What does an Indian Agent do?"

She smiled as they began the waltz. He danced more elegantly than she had immediately supposed from his somewhat hesitant formal bearing.

"An Indian Agent is the only person disposed and certainly officially obliged to defend Indian interests. I am therefore hated on objective terms by nearly everyone. This obliges me to be as ingratiating on personal terms as I can. Clearly a split purpose which entails great risk of failure on both counts and practically no likelihood of resounding success."

"That is a most curious occupation. How did you come to it?"

"I was raised in Philadelphia. Not in itself an explanation, but we are an old Quaker family comfortably settled in reassuring rhetorical commitment to the betterment of mankind. As a boy I spent summers on a ranch in the Dakotas just east of here. I got to know the Indians and learned their language. Later I acquired a missionary zeal to right the wrongs we have done them. Such tiresome moralism struck my family as rather odd, but I couched it in such traditional Quaker terms they could hardly oppose. They did insist that I finish college, then try the Indian Agent job for a year or so. It has nearly been two years."

All this time Philip had been swirling Amanda proficiently in a somewhat breathtaking waltz that induced mild exhilaration, something she had not experienced since embassy parties in India. Suddenly they were startled by gunfire some distance from the pavilion. Amanda looked at Philip in alarm.

"Nothing to worry about although it does seem a bit out of place. They are probably skeet shooting. Some people can't let a day go by without shooting something I guess that's my nonviolent upbringing talking."

"I agree with you. I was horrified coming out here on the train to see them slaughter the buffalo. Absolutely to no purpose. Just killing for the sake of killing."

"I tried to get legislation to protect the buffalo, but no one cared, least of all the ranchers who see them taking grazing from their herds. Would you care for some refreshment?"

They walked to the buffet table where Lord Basil was standing, unable to choose a dance partner among the ranchers' wives with whom he was chatting. More couples began to dance, creating heavy traffic around the dance floor. Perhaps because she was so beautiful, not to say formidable, Ariadne had been instinctively neglected by the gentlemen present. Not that they wouldn't like to dance with her, but unable to formulate an opening line to such a proposal. Brandon noticed that she was abandoned to the company of two rather senior wives and walked over.

"Excuse me Miss, may I have the great pleasure of this dance?"

He produced as bullet-proof a smile as Ariadne had ever seen, startlingly white teeth, against his tanned leathery skin. His deep blue eyes flashed brilliantly, such that, for a change, it was she who was taken aback as her admirers usually were. She didn't say anything, simply lifted her hand, under which he placed his arm, and they turned to the floor and began to dance. His silence induced an awkward uncharacteristic silence in her, as if she were under the influence of some alien force intimidating her faculty of speech. He held her firmly and danced elegantly, but was by no means forward or inappropriate in his conduct. She enjoyed letting him lead the dance and began to relax under his assured direction, as bringing momentary welcome relief from the effort to maintain a critical presence of mind. They danced in absolute silence for several minutes. Then her wonted orneriness began to recover, and she began to interpret his silence more as weakness than strength, her inclination to verbal cleverness making her especially mocking of anyone who could not reciprocate.

"Well, you are the Great Stone Face! I have never spent this much time in such proximity to anyone to whom I have neither spoken nor been introduced."

She shook her curls and looked up at him. He showed his large happy teeth and no sign of intimidation or interest, which increased her aggravation. But he was not so uncivil as to remain silent in the face of her perfectly fair expectation of conversation.

"I was struck so dumb by your beauty that I let my manners lapse. I am Brandon Evans, employed as manager of Mr. Braddock's ranch. He lets me dance with the prettiest girls whenever there is a party and I agree not to run off to California."

"How extraordinary. You mean to tell me I am the only thing standing in the way of your departure for California?"

"For the moment."

He smiled back at her and resumed a vigorous waltz. They danced in competition now, she is driving the dance harder and he in turn responding while keeping the lead. The band finally stopped, and they stood and clapped for a moment.

"May I escort you for some refreshment? Braddock usually provides amply for his guests."

She nodded and they walked to the buffet table. Lord Basil had observed their dancing with mixed feelings. He realized his social lapse in not rushing to engage his fiancée in the first dance. On the other hand, he was relieved not to have to endure her repartée and mercurial moods, especially where they could erupt publicly. He had acquired a kind of fear of her wild spirit and her formidable physical beauty, which now seemed all the more dangerous, unconstrained by the context of stately home, servants, social protocols, schedules, and formalities. At Leasworth Castle in Kent he could preside over an establishment that reinforced, even augmented his person. Here, in the middle of nowhere, without structure or a modicum of respect for form, he felt diminished, vulnerable, as if waking from a nightmare dressed as a bank clerk with no one who knew him or much cared what happened to him.

Ariadne, contrariwise, was just beginning to sense the relief such absence of form and social constraint might bring. Not that she would wish to give up the elegance of Leasworth Castle and the endless opportunities wealth and prominence of title would provide. Lord Basil was simply one of the necessary furnishings for so splendid a life she was obliged to acquire requisite to possession of more attractive resources. She had not formulated her feelings in quite this candid way before, but the greater liberty and lack of bounds the American west seemed to offer, gave greater scope to her infinite capacity to test and provoke what she instinctively disapproved and even found physically repellant.

In the waning afternoon of a Colorado summer, Lord Basil appeared distinctly less fetching than he had on the lawn of Leasworth Castle just two months before. Whether it was the fact that he could not draw strength from a sense of proprietorship in surroundings bound to impress all who observed them, or whether he had simply begun to feel the effects of a long and tedious journey, he appeared rather pale, weak, and unhealthy, perhaps the worst thing in Ariadne's eyes. She covertly compared him to Brandon Evans' rather solid large and handsome presence, and ruled in favor of the latter. She led Brandon to Lord Basil with malice of intent he would have no way of anticipating.

"Dear Basil, I want you to meet my new cowboy friend Brandon Evans. He rustles cattle for a living. Brandon, this is my fiancé Lord Basil Pomeroy, who has no occupation at all but might find yours of some interest."

She turned abruptly and left the two men, startled and in a mutually sympathetic lurch.

"Pleased to meet you, Lord Basil. You have my sympathy. With such a ferocious fiancée to manage I imagine you are fully occupied as it is without taking on other obligations. I admit I would take a ranch any day to tackling a bronco as unruly as Ariadne."

Lord Basil was delighted by the remark and the comradeship implied, having doubted at first the likelihood of his engaging this rather rough-looking character in any way agreeably.

"Brilliant analysis of my predicament, Sir. And I am exceedingly glad to meet you. If I may presume, I should like to see much of you in the weeks ahead. Experience in managing large herds of unruly cattle should qualify you to advise me on the proper means of subduing my prospective bride."

He laughed and shook Brandon's hand. The skeet shooting continued, and Brandon suggested they see how it was going. They caught up with Ariadne and together they walked some fifty yards to where a target shoot was under way beyond a small grove of trees that muffled the sound and kept it away so far as possible the barns and the skittish horses and cattle. By this time nearly all the guests had gathered to watch to contestants. Colonel Drake fired his Colt .45. Sheriff Westmorland drawn to the contest by several men who knew they detested each other. The skeet thrower was Garrison VanDuesen, a New York banker friend of Braddock. Father Allen Montescue stood talking to three senior wives, while Braddock and Sir Charles Winthrop discussed business with several ranch owners. Whenever a skeet went up they all stopped and waited for the shot, then applauded politely. Someone shouted at Philip who had accompanied Amanda to the contest.

"Philip! Get over there and show them how it should be done."

Philip was a crack shot but observed the Quaker abhorrence of violence and especially guns. He did carry a rifle when riding in the wild lands for hunting and self-defense, but he went unarmed around town and at the reservation. A group of guests began to ride him, insisting that he take a few shots. Amanda smiled at him encouragingly.

"All right, but you know I can't outshoot these two."

He went to the shooting line and took up a rifle. Garrison threw a skeet off to the right. Philip easily hit it. Colonel Drake sensing growing excitement and noticing the arrival of Lord Basil and Ariadne, suggested they try more difficult shots. The crowd roared approval and it was agreed the skeet thrower move out thirty yards, standing behind two trees for protection. He would throw the skeet while Drake, Westmoreland and Philip tuned their backs. He would then shout, and the men would turn and fire.

"That's how we picked off Johnny Reb."

Drake flashed a wicked smile at the wives gathered in fascinated horror behind him and the Sheriff. They were now shooting with such rapidity at such random difficult skeet throws, no one could understand how they could hit the clay disks at all. At fifty to seventy-five yards, a four-inch diameter disk was hardly larger than a silver dollar to the eye of Mrs. Framingham, wife of a prominent Wall Street banker whose ample paunch was gratefully digesting the fried chicken with salsa sauce he had devoured before joining the shooting match. Whatever exertions in the line of fitness he had come to Colorado to pursue had apparently been indefinitely postponed. The men laughed at Drake's remark, all except Westmoreland who did not visibly react to Drake's comment although his eyes narrowed as he looked at him. Drake figured that if his remark could anger the Sheriff, he might fire just a bit too soon or miscalculate the lead just enough to lose a shot.

Even demonstrations of astonishing accuracy, if protracted, begin to pall and the guests soon lost interest. After half an hour Drake and Westmoreland returned to the party. It was twilight and oil lamps had been lit around the pavilion and throughout the grounds, giving a warm bacchanalian glow as the sky grew darker. The makeshift band played waltzes, polkas, and Mexican dances. As night wore on the party became livelier under the influence of champagne and whisky combined deceptively in a punch that led even the women to drink more than might be prudent. Couplings furtively imagined in the minds of respectable wives became impulsively potential. Couples danced vigorously in the dramatically flickering light of the oil lamps. Ariadne danced with Brandon in almost a gallop around the pavilion, she for the moment at least engaged enjoyably to all appearances. Philip approached Amanda.

"I'd like you to meet Leah Featherstone. She's the daughter of the owner of the general store. Lovely girl. Her mother was Cherokee. Such a gentle sensitive girl, I thought you would enjoy her company."

"I'd be delighted to meet her. Is her mother not alive?"

"She died of typhus. Leah and her father cater these parties. Leah is over there at the refreshment table serving punch."

They left the pavilion and approached the refreshment table.

"Leah. I'd like you to meet Amanda Egerton, our guest from England."

Leah smiled shyly, searching Amanda's face. Amanda smiled back and between them passed that unspoken bond of immediate liking between two kindred spirits.

"Leah and I are going to be great friends. I feel it already."

They talked together for a few minutes when there was a commotion from the pavilion. Amanda looked up to see Ariadne, flushed and rushing from the dance floor. Brandon moved after her a few steps, then gave it up and walked off toward the stables. The other dancers looked at them reprovingly for a moment then resumed dancing, since the band already well supplied with punch was playing oblivious to what happened. Amanda considered following Ariadne, but decided she would likely be able to take care of herself. What exactly happened between her, and Brandon was unknown, but temperamental outbursts were not exceptional for Ariadne and by now those who knew her were less likely to take them quite as the world-shaking events they might appear to be to outsiders or herself for that matter.

Ariadne had not spoken to Lord Basil all evening. As she rushed from the pavilion, she spotted him with the French wife of her host's neighbor and walked toward him.

"Do forgive me Mrs. Vanneuve. I really must get reacquainted with my fiancé. It has been ages since we last met."

"Of course, I understand parfaitement. He is so charming, you should keep closer watch over him."

Ariadne led Lord Basil off toward the main house. Once inside she quickly ran upstairs with him following awkwardly behind. The upstairs hall was unoccupied. She led him down the hall to her suite. He withdrew at the door, but she insisted, laughing.

"On come on silly. We're engaged. You're entitled to take liberties."

She shut the door. The full moon cast silver light over the dressing table, the Queen Anne chairs, the bureau and side tables. In the adjoining room the large canopy bed was equally lit by the moth-wing moonlight. She moved up close to him.

"Kiss me Basil, I insist."

"You are so extraordinary Ariadne. However...."

He touched his lips to hers very lightly and looked up.

"There! That is quite sufficient and well within the bound of honor and respect with which I esteem you."

He smiled a reproachful smile. She had on previous occasions engaged in such capricious and provoking behavior. The first time he was mildly flattered, never having been so physically assaulted by a woman. But subsequent occasions became discomfiting, as though some wild uncivil rule lay beneath her lively, teasing manner. Ariadne felt a welling of frustration, largely prompted by her dancing with Brandon, arousing a passion she had never fulfilled. Observing Lord Basil, anger, even contempt quickly redirected to bantering remarks, a growing and unresolved need driving her to provoke him as he so obviously shrank from her.

"No. It is not sufficient. I want you to really kiss me. Just to see how it feels. Here, give me your hand."

He offered his hand. She took it, lowered the front of her dress and placed his hand on her breasts.

"There, feel my body."

She said it with a yearning, wanting look, appealing to him. Her heart was pounding, and her nipples firmed with excitement.

"Really Ariadne, I simply cannot condone this. I will not betray the trust of Sir Charles."

He confusedly withdrew his hand and looked away from her bare breasts. She flared angrily.

"Well, what in God's name will you do when we are married? Don't you have any red blood in your veins? Can't you see I'm a woman?"

Her anger gave him an advantage that he had not had when subject to her humorous taunts.

"I will love you and honor you as the lovely wife you will be."

He lifted her hand, kissed it and left the room. She stood leaning against the door, arching her back, feeling swelling desire run through her body, seeing her nipples erect in the light of the beckoning moon.

Sir Basil returned to the stair well, flustered, perturbed, excited, upset. He felt humiliated, inadequate, out of his depth. Her conduct was inexcusable, yet somehow, he felt he was in the wrong. He reached the top of the stairs when Raymond approached from the other wing of the house.

"Oh, hello Basil. I was just up for a minute. You look rather unwell. Is anything the matter?"

"No. Just a bit of the heat and champagne. I just accompanied Ariadne to her room. She wasn't feeling well and wanted to turn in."

The lie helped calm his nerves. Raymond took him by the arm.

"I think you need some rest yourself. Let me get you to your room."

"Well perhaps you are right. I do feel rather down."

They walked to the end of the corridor opposite the one in which women guests were quartered. Raymond opened the door and Lord Basil went in. Raymond shut the door and followed him.

"Tell me about it, Basil. Is it Ariadne?"

Raymond spoke the words in nearly a whisper. He put his arm around Lord Basil and moved him to the sofa where they sat side by side. The months of confusion and worry about Ariadne's expectations seemed to fuse into a feeling of desperation. Lord Basil spoke, as much to himself as to Raymond, trying to sort out his feelings and especially his fears.

"I really am not sure it is likely to work. She is so…immediate, and I obviously am not able to match whatever expectations she has."

He looked at Raymond with pleading eyes. Raymond spoke softly.

"I understand Basil. I want you to know how close I feel to you. I am deeply unhappy at your distress. If there is anything I can do to help you I will gladly do it."

He leaned across and kissed Lord Basil on the mouth. Lord Basil, relieved by his friend's support and tender kiss, suddenly acknowledged a feeling of closeness and desire that earlier he had not been able to interpret or understand. He leaned toward Raymond with a new realization.

Braddock, Sir Charles and Lord Basil spent nearly ten days in their travels to and from the mining camp. They rode west on horseback and arrived at the camp toward the evening of the second day. The mining engineers were prepared to brief them on the current findings, but Lord Basil was so exhausted they postponed the meeting to the following morning. Albert Searle, chief engineer, explained the use of electromagnetic soundings using dynamite to plot geologic formations in the area. Some looked promising, others not. He could not personally guarantee success. Mineral deposits were a gamble at all times. He looked professional, skeptical, wore round, metal-rimmed glasses, lace-up boots, and riding breeches, a khaki shirt with pockets full of pencils. Braddock thought such an academic looking fellow would be useful in attracting investors, no push or excitement to arouse suspicion about the prospects. A hint of scientific skepticism might whet the appetite of jaded investors accustomed to sales pitches and likely to suspect unqualified confidence in the venture.

Searle had his assistant Gregory Bates explain the new technology used to plot geologic formations. Seismic testing using electronic sensors that measure wave responses sounded more convincing than trotting out jars of ore samples or divining rod estimates. Braddock decided he would bring these two with him to New York in September. Sir Charles was impressed as well. Clearly a combination of scientific mumbo jumbo, ore samples, electronic data, and a moderately optimistic sales pitch would give this project legs in the market. The growing need for copper in telegraph, electric and rail industries suggested unlimited demand. By-products of gold and silver would simply grease the wheels.

Lord Basil on the other hand was losing whatever interest he once had. The west was getting him down, the food rudimentary, the landscape unrelieved, the people unimpressive, and his engagement to Ariadne increasingly unpromising. That they would be an impossible combination was apparent to both. Saddle sores are an added contributor to disillusion. He had traveled at his father's insistence to acquaint himself with investment opportunities, thereby to prepare him for association with Imperial Bank and to seal the bond between himself, Ariadne, and Sir Charles. The whole thing had been a kind of corporate merger of economic interest, estate management and personal gratification. Now he foresaw no gratification and little interest, despite the wealth Sir Charles could bring to his title and estate of large, entailed properties expensive to maintain. For the rest of the trip, Lord Basil remained taciturn, outwardly agreeable, inwardly rebellious.

The party returned to the Double-B ranch two days later than expected. After dinner the first night back, Braddock and Sir Charles withdrew to the library for a game of billiards.

"Too bad your engineers' report shows promising deposits of copper and silver only on the Indian reservation. This needn't present an insuperable difficulty, but it will require some careful staging."

Sir Charles sank a ball in the side pocket and stood up.

"I should think the Indians matter little when such stakes are in play."

Braddock reviewed his choices. He could play a bank shot for ten points or take a safer shot in the corner pocket for four points. He went for the ten.

"It was bad enough when these New England matrons adopted the negroes and forced a civil war on us. They now want to stop the advance of the frontier by granting Indians 'inalienable rights'. But most people want growth and settlement and won't stand for much Indian nonsense."

His ball banked perfectly and sank two others. Sir Charles raised his eyebrows in admiration.

"What sort of 'staging' are you talking about?"

"We need to create an incident that justifies driving the Indians off their reservation. This used to be a lot easier, but the newspapers have taken to discovering such plots and exposing them, so it becomes difficult to buy politicians' support. I think we can work with Colonel Drake to arrange

something convincing. So long as the Army is involved, we should be able to carry it off."

Sir Charles in turn sank a difficult bank shot, reinforcing their mutual regard.

"From what you tell me, Colonel Drake is a rather rum fellow. What's his story?"

"He attended West Point but didn't graduate. Too many southerners who also ran the regular Army to compete successfully. He went into business, like Grant. Rejoined in 1861 and made Brigadier General temporary promotion. Like Custer, a close friend of his. Drake was wounded at Chattanooga. Never entirely recovered, mentally or physically. Rather bitter man, not very healthy I should say, although he carries out his duties well enough. He has a frontier rabble of alcoholic war veterans, Irish immigrants, fugitives. Hardly matches your idea of an Army."

"Whatever his personal problems, can we rely on him is what counts."

"Oh, he's reliable enough. An absolute Indian hater, the first qualification. Also, a fighter. And what's more important, a dirty fighter. He would have no scruples about ambushing the Indians or killing their women and children. He volunteered to lead marauder battalions in the war. He had no qualms over slash and burn and slaughter. Not someone you want in your club, but certainly useful in your firm."

Sir Charles sank a ball in the side pocket, smiled at his victory, lifted his glass of champagne, and said:

"Here's to Drake!"

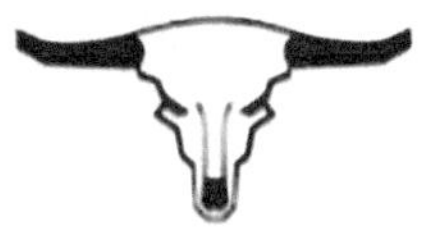

Amanda entered the general store, pleasantly surprised by the scents of spice, oats, dry goods, the mellow light playing across wooden handles, barrels of apples, the glass-paned showcase with an array of candy, licorice sticks red and black, the soft light from the store front windows spreading a welcoming warmth. She didn't notice the girl behind the counter until she was quite close. Leah looked expectantly, shyly, at the well-dressed stranger, who in turn looked kindly at her and with some surprise.

"Oh, I'm sorry. I didn't notice you before. I was so absorbed in admiring the store."

Leah nodded thanks and smiled. Her open trusting eyes obviously excited to find Amanda so gentle and friendly. Amanda was immediately attracted to Leah, her long hair, soft brown eyes, looking so young, vulnerable and lovely. She held out her hand.

"You and I must be friends. Since I am new to town and have no others, we will be best friends if you like."

Leah beamed shyly, took Amanda's hand. She became excited in the way people do when they meet kindred spirits, eager to remain close to the new person, to prolong as long as possible the wonderful moment of discovery.

"May I show you anything in particular. We have some new fabrics from Chicago, just arrived."

"Yes. Show me the fabrics. I probably will need something much lighter to wear than what I brought with me. It is so much warmer here than in England where I come from."

Leah came from behind the counter. Amanda followed her to the back of the store, where bolts of calico, muslin, wool, cotton and linen were arrayed on a shelf. Together they tested the weight, texture and color of each one. They agreed that three were best suited to Amanda.

"I would be happy to sew a dress for you if you like."

"That's lovely of you. But I can't have you do that for me without my doing something for you. If you are willing, I would like to go riding with you so you can show me the country hereabouts. I can provide the horses. I also want to be with my new friend as much as possible, and I can't go shopping everyday as you can imagine."

Leah said she would love to go riding, that she has her own horse, and would ask her father, who was in their living quarters upstairs. She ran upstairs and, in a few minutes, Featherstone appeared smiling graciously, if a little quizzically, having little experience of wealthy easterners taking an interest in his daughter. More to the contrary, there had been a distinct reluctance to be more than minimally polite to Leah, likely reflecting the discomfort that mixed race progeny inspired in the phalanx of respectable white matrons. But he saw immediately that Amanda harbored no such bias toward Leah. They talked about the store, and Amanda spoke about how suddenly both she and Leah found they were kindred spirits and how she would very much like to go riding about the country with Leah. Leah was an expert horsewoman. Amanda assured Featherstone that she had ridden horses from India to Sudan to England and could handle them well enough.

The first ride was agreed to for the day after tomorrow, Amanda offered to bring a horse, but Leah preferred to ride her Appaloosa, called Peanut. Amanda took her hand before leaving the store, said goodbye to Featherstone, and then impulsively kissed Leah on the cheek, whereupon Leah blushed, and her eyes filled with tears. Amanda was so touched that her eyes filled with tears as well, tears of joy and wonder and happiness that the bond that had started with mutual affinity began to grow richer and more profound in ways that neither could consciously explain. Amanda returned to the ranch with a lightness of heart she had not felt since the death of her father two years before.

Two days later Amanda rode to town and met Leah. At Leah's suggestion they rode to the river that twined around for miles as if reluctant to reach the point of merger with her big brother the Mississippi. Here and there in the wide oxbows were huddles of cottonwood and willows along its banks. Leah showed Amanda her favorite spot, unknown or at least not used by anyone else so far as she could tell.

"I come here sometimes just for the peace. The birds sing so sweetly, and the water just bubbles by so gently. It's even nice to swim."

Amanda breathed deeply as they led the horses into the cluster of trees. Under the canopy it was remarkably cool and the bright hard light of the mid-afternoon sun was muted by the light-green leaves. Leah set out blankets at the base of a cottonwood tree and they sat down.

"You swim here? In the river?"

"Yes, of course. I make sure no one is anywhere in sight and I stay down in the water."

Amanda looked a bit shocked.

"You mean you swim…without any clothes on?"

Leah looked embarrassed.

"I'm sorry if I sound shocked Leah. Now that I think about it, it makes perfect sense. I wish I could swim with you."

Leah smiled and said they could do so sometime. They sat on the blankets and watched the whip-poor-wills (their song sounded like that) and blackbirds vying for their attention. The river gurgled pale green/blue green under the bright blue sky. White puffs of cloud very high above drifted lazily by, a light breeze moved through the branches. They lay back on the blankets. Leah looked dreamily at Amanda.

"Miss Amanda, what is England like?"

"Oh, it is quite different than here, Leah. Large cities with too many people. Very noisy, except for the countryside where there is peace and quiet, but I don't think it ever gets as nice as it is here among the trees."

She smiled at Leah who smiled back, pleased that this place was special for Amanda too. After a time, Amanda suddenly turned to Leah and said in an enthusiastic impetuous voice she had not heard herself use in years.

"Let's go swimming!"

"Oh yes, let's! It's so cool and refreshing."

They both laughed and got up to undress. Leah's light tan body was lithe and beautiful under the dappled light of the trees. Amanda had never before undressed in any place remotely public before, but a new feeling of energy and excitement coursed through her body, a brief moment of self-consciousness immediately overcome by a sense of freedom and exhilaration she often felt when riding with her father in India.

Amanda's pale body, also lithe and beautiful, contrasted with the nut-brown color of Leah's. They laughed as Leah took her hand and led her to the riverbank. A dense cluster of willows created a sheltered area into which they could enter the river. The water was cool and clear, the turbulence of spring runoff long past. They dipped down full into the water.

"I'm not a very good swimmer, Leah. I probably would sink like a lead weight if I get in over my head."

"Don't worry Miss Amanda, it's not very deep. Even in the middle we can stand with our heads above water. Here, I'll show you."

She swam out into the sunlight and stood some twenty yards from shore. Amanda waded out ten yards and then swam out to Leah. The current was noticeable but not strong, enough to move her downstream slowly as she swam, so she compensated by heading upstream. They splashed around and laughed together, enjoying the warmth of the sun in contrast to the cool water. After about half an hour they headed back to shore. They stood under the trees, as a light warm breeze dried their bodies.

"That was wonderful, Leah. I'm so glad we are friends. Can we do this again sometime?"

Leah beamed joyfully. She had never had a friend before. She was deeply in love with Amanda and would do anything for her. Instead of speaking, Leah impulsively hugged Amanda and kissed her cheek, then stepped back, looked shocked at her behavior, hoping Amanda was not offended. Amanda laughed, hugged and kissed her in return, love welling up between them from their shared early loss of their mothers and their need for a feminine bond that would in some way fill the emptiness they had suffered as a result. They stood side by side, naked in the filtered sunlight among the cottonwoods, arms around each other, looking at the river through the willows. The glorious sun, endless blue sky, smiling white clouds far, far above gave them a sense of peace and belonging they had never felt before in their young lives.

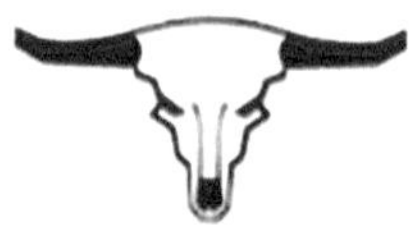

Ariadne dressed for her daily ride and walked to the stables. Brandon had saddled her horse and stood holding the reins. She moved quickly toward the horse, hardly looked at Brandon, tossing her hair, swinging her arms decisively.

He smiled his invincible smile, gave her a hearty *"Good morning!"* The first week she muttered 'good morning', put her boot in the stirrup, swung quickly into the saddle, and trotted off briskly. As the ritual of the daily ride went on, she said nothing. After Sir Charles and Lord Basil had been gone two days longer than expected, she was especially irritable. This morning Brandon greeted her as usual.

"For God's sake, stop saying good morning and lose that insufferable smile!"

He laughed as she galloped off, the sight of her poised, beautifully arched back, gracious figure handily astride the brown mare stabbed his heart. Since she stormed off at the party they had not conversed, despite their daily encounters. His attempts at conversation were simply ignored. He gave it up as a lost cause.

Two days later the mare needed a shoe. He was in the stable nailing it on when she stormed in. The mid-morning heat was stifling. Shafts of sunlight lit the haunches of horses in their bays, the troughs of oats, the straw strewn over the ground. The mountain of hay piled at the back of the stable was golden in the indirect light, gave off an intoxicating smell mixed with the pungent odor of horses.

Brandon stood half lit in darkness, naked to the waist in the oppressive heat. He had removed his shirt and was wet with sweat, his powerful chest deeply tanned. She walked up to him and stood quietly for a moment, looking into his eyes. Then she slapped his face with all the strength she could muster. Her body throbbed and she felt dizzy. He reached for her, pulled her gently toward himself, and kissed her softly. She struggled and pushed him away, but he held her firmly, kissed her again more urgently. She began to respond, kissing his mouth in ways she had never done before, as if some instinct were taking over inside of her. Her body pressed against him. He pulled down her riding skirt, kneaded her buttocks, moved his firm gentle hand between her legs. She groaned and spread her legs to give him more access. She tore open her blouse and bustier and pressed her bare breasts against his chest, rubbing them against the sweaty black hair. He had released his penis and worked it into her, his head swimming, pulsing blindly dizzily. She was virgin, but he moved into her firmly and tenderly. She felt pain and then release as it entered fully, as if her entire being was finally where it belonged. He stroked her steadily in slow thrusts, enjoying the welling pleasure of the buildup as she breathed heavily in short gasps. He hungrily kissed her mouth. She opened hers and they trust their tongues into each other trying to achieve the greatest possible merger of their bodies. He now lost all control, letting passion take over, thrusting firmly and with greater speed in a smooth urgent rhythm. She groaned and gasped '*Yes, yes*', as she relished her maidenhead taken by this strong virile man. As she came, he released a flood of semen into her soft lovely body, thrust after thrust pouring a fountain of love and passion into her as the horses snorted and shuffled uneasily in their stalls, aware in some way of the deep primitive force that joined them all in the wild dance of life.

Despite the full moon, the area immediately behind the general store was pitch dark. Potshot Brand had dragged a ladder under the second-floor window and carefully set it against the wall of the house.

He concentrated hard to keep as quiet as possible. He climbed the rungs slowly. There was nothing behind the building as far as you could see, which was quite far in the open moonlight. The window curtains were pulled aside, since Leah had no reason to suppose anyone could see into her room.

Potshot carefully edged himself to the window and very slowly positioned himself so he could see inside. Leah was seated on a chair reading in a corner of the room. It was about eleven o'clock. He had observed Leah for over a week and figured he didn't have long to wait before she started getting ready for bed. In about ten minutes Leah got up and began to undress. She removed her skirt, folded it, and placed it on the seat of a chair. She unbuttoned her blouse and draped it over the back of the chair. She pulled her slip over her head, tossing her long hair as she straightened up. She removed her underwear and folded it neatly on top of her skirt. In the candlelight her body looked as chaste and lithe as a fawn. She went to her dresser and got her nightgown, slipped it over her head. Show over.

Potshot (a nickname he acquired for reasons long forgotten) quietly descended the ladder, carried it into the field and concealed it in the high bunchgrass. He had stalked Leah for several weeks, obsessed by her quiet dignity, the beauty of her long dark hair, the light tan of her complexion heightened by the warm rose of her cheeks. He sometimes went to the general store just to see her distributing stock or doing chores, until she became embarrassed and went into the back of the store. Potshot walked back to the saloon and ordered whisky. He remembered Leah's creamy skin, the long black hair. He counted the $20 gold coins in his pocket. Alison Faraday brought drinks to some soldiers seated at a table near the saloon doors. Brady played the piano, Elvira tended bar. Five cowboys played poker at another table, a few lone drinkers along the bar stared into their glasses, occasionally joked with Elvira. Melinda, a mulatto, with large brown eyes and café-au-lait skin sat at a table in a corner of the saloon nursing a whisky and talking to three soldiers. She wore a low-cut dress that showed her large breasts. She was otherwise rather lean, waif-like, with narrow hips and long lean legs and arms. Potshot walked over and put three $20 gold coins on the table beside her. The soldiers stopped talking. She took a sip of whisky, ignored the money. Potshot smiled.

"So, let's go."

"No way."

Potshot's smile died a slow death on his face. His stocky body stiffened.

"Let's go. Here's the money."

Melinda looked away from him, smiling at one of the soldiers, Andrew Pike, blond, about twenty-years old, nice looking farm kid she took a liking to.

"I said no way. Not you, not ever!"

Potshot's neck reddened, his jaw muscles clenched, his eyes narrowed under his thick black eyebrows.

"Let's go nigger."

Melinda flushed angrily, her eyes flashed at him.

"Don't call me nigger, you white trash bastard. Get out of here and leave me alone…with these gentlemen."

Her manner changed entirely as she turned and smiled at the three soldiers, who shifted in their chairs sensing trouble, not sure which way things would go. Andrew had drunk a few whiskeys and felt chivalrous. Melinda struck some romantic chord. She did sell her favors, but her manner always suggested that she did the choosing, based on how well she liked the man, so it seemed more personal than transactional.

"Hey mister, leave the lady alone. She doesn't want to be bothered."

Potshot turned toward Andrew.

"Stay out of this kid. She's a whore and I'm paying. Let's go!"

Andrew stood up. He was tall, strong, but maybe not a street fighter. Potshot took a chance and shot a fist into his stomach. Andrew doubled up. The other two soldiers stood up, pulled Andrew back. Melinda screamed at Potshot. The men along the bar sidled over to the table, Elvira and Mandy came over, Brady stopped playing. Melinda ran over to Andrew and held his face in her hands.

"Baby, if that son of a bitch hurt you, I'll cut his fucking guts out."

She kissed Andrew, who regained his breath and stood up.

"Let's go outside mister."

Potshot sized him up again, then walked toward the swinging doors, slowly. The others followed onto the street, formed a circle, encouraged Andrew, while Melinda continued swearing at Potshot. Potshot and Andrew took off their shirts. Potshot was heavier but Andrew had broad shoulders and longer reach. They sparred for a few seconds, then Potshot threw a left uppercut that grazed Andrew's chin. Andrew fell back, regained his footing just as Potshot moved up to him. Andrew sliced a right to the side of Potshot's face. It didn't land with full force, but it did drive Potshot backward. Potshot feigned a right, threw a left, then tried to trip Andrew. Trying to trip him enraged Andrew. He began throwing punches rapidly as Potshot tried to duck and move under Andrew's arms to attack his stomach. Potshot sent a side kick at Andrew, trying to force him back, further enraging Andrew. Andrew threw a left uppercut that struck Potshot full force, he stumbled, and Andrew threw a right to the jaw, knocking him down. The crowd cheered as Potshot spun around in the dirt trying to get away from Andrew, who was bleeding from nose and mouth and smiling grotesquely. Some cowboys moved in and separated them.

They walked Andrew back to the saloon, leaving Potshot lying in the street. Melinda ordered two whiskeys, dipped the hem of her dress in one, and began daubing Andrew's nose and lip. She smiled radiantly at him, her Galahad, and he grinned at her, still a bit dopey. He tossed back the other glass of whisky, choked, and then laughed. Brady back at the piano started *Oh! Susanna* and the cowboys and soldiers began singing at the top of their voices. Whisky flowed. Elvira and Mandy were busy handing out drinks. Several soldiers and cowboys went outside to fire off a few rounds just to relieve their feelings. After about half an hour, Melinda and Andrew walked unsteadily upstairs, as the crowd cheered and laughed. Andrew waved victoriously from the top landing. Potshot stood, silent and alone, in the street, listening.

Indian traders visited the Double-B ranch. An elderly squaw displayed handmade jewelry, silver and turquoise and agate bracelets, necklaces, rings. Amanda found them ravishing and bought several, including a particularly lovely scarab necklace in silver with beautifully luminous turquoise. The next day she and Leah rode to their secret refuge. Amanda put the necklace around Leah's neck after their swim. Leah burst into tears, hugged Amanda, and told her she loved her and that being her friend was the most wonderful thing that ever happened to her. They both cried in each other's arms for a while, and then began to laugh together as two conspirators joyfully linked in a cosmic trick played on the World. Leah, the half-breed Indian girl from Oklahoma, and Amanda, the last survivor of the Egerton family that had provided warriors, justices, and landlords in Hampshire County since Edward III.

Two weeks later Amanda sent word to Leah that she couldn't go on their usual ride, was bitterly disappointed, and would come to town the following day for a visit to make up for it. Leah was also disappointed but happy that she would see her friend the next day. She debated whether to tell her father and then decided she would ride out on her own as she had done before she met Amanda. The day was unusually hot, with no relief in sight. She rode along the riverbank to her favorite stand of cottonwoods and willows. Under the trees the air was cooler. She undressed and entered the river. It was an immense relief from the blistering sun. Even in midstream she had to keep ducking into the water to offset the nearly unbearable heat. She swam for a while and then went back into the grove, lying on the blanket while she dried. In the heat, after the swim, she felt drowsy and fell asleep.

Potshot sat under trees on the opposite bank of the river, tugging at a bottle of whisky, still nursing his grievance over the fight of a week before. The humiliation of the fight combined with Melinda's refusal to go with him rankled. He was drowsy and hardly cared if he caught any fish. He liked to nap in the cottonwoods along the river, the only place offering relief from the heat. He rarely rode this far out of town, but he had been so preoccupied by the wounds to his ego and drowsy from the whisky as he rode under the blazing sun, that he traveled much farther from town than he intended. He spotted the trees ahead and figured he would stay there until sunset.

It was with some amazement that he saw through the willows Leah enter the river on the opposite bank. Brought fully alert, he stared at her as she paddled around in the water, diving and curling around like a mermaid, showing the lean tan length of her body glistening in the sunlight. He became so excited that he nearly dropped his bottle. He took several more swigs and rubbed his eyes. Leah swam a while and then went back to shore. So far as he could tell, she remained in the grove.

The river wasn't deep in mid-summer. He decided it was worth trying to cross just to see if she was still there. He took off his gun belt, boots and shirt, stuck his knife in his pants belt and quietly waded into the water under cover of the willows. He kept his head just above water. He took his time, trying not to make any noise. He headed upstream from where he saw her enter the grove, and touched shore just above the cluster of cottonwoods. As quietly as he could, despite the intense sun and dizziness caused by the whisky, he crept toward the grove. He entered the shade of the trees and saw Leah asleep on the blanket at the foot of the largest cottonweed. Although nude, she looked chaste as some water nymph gently napping in an Arcadian paradise. She was so innocent and lovely that even he stopped and simply looked at her beauty without lust or prurience, so gaspingly beautiful she was. But his memory of spying on her undressing and the erotic arousal that memory of the movement of her body inspired, sent blood rushing to his groin and head in a blood lust especially charged by the fact that he had never seen any woman as beautiful as Leah. He moved toward her and, as if by some perverse logic that her present nudity implied consent, he said roughly:

"Damn, you are something to see!"

Leah opened her eyes uncomprehending, then terrified. She moved violently to escape. He grabbed her as he fell on her. She struggled with all her strength, nearly turning him over. She was silent at first, then began to scream. He felt her body against his bare chest. He forced her hands behind her back and held them with his left hand as he undid his pants and released his inflamed penis. She kicked and moved her knees as violently as she could, partly catching him in the groin. He moaned and nearly released his grip. She was almost free when he pulled his knife and stabbed her in the side. She groaned but kept struggling. He stabbed her in the stomach. She weakened enough that her knees stopped striking him up and down. He moved between her legs, forcing himself inside her. She was bleeding profusely over both of them, he groaned hoarsely. He finally broke into her and wildly began stroking, his stinking whisky breath and rancid sweat filling her nostrils. She moaned:

"No no no...."

He kept pumping into her, reached climax, and dropped exhausted at her side. All the struggle in her body stopped. After some minutes he got up. She was dead. Horribly mangled. He saw the necklace and pulled it from her neck. He felt for her heartbeat. There was none. He picked up the knife, stumbled toward the river, and threw it far downstream. He could wash the blood off, and no one would suspect he had murdered her. He rubbed his body and pants for several minutes. He then waded to the opposite shore, crawled into the grove and lay down for an hour to rest. The blood was washed off his pants and body. He put on his shirt, gathered up his tackle, and headed out of the trees to his horse. It was only five miles back to town, but he took an alternate route so he wouldn't be seen by any stray travelers. He got back to town after dark and went to the shed he slept in. He put the necklace in his pack and went to sleep, but began to shake and had to wait nearly an hour before finally dropping off. He reassured himself that with any luck at all, no one would ever know.

Featherstone began counting the day's take. It was sunset and Leah had not returned from her ride. He was concerned but assumed that she had been delayed at the Double-B ranch with Amanda. Still, she always returned by six o'clock before and he thought he might ride out to the ranch to see if they were still there. Philip entered the store to buy provisions. He selected what he wanted, and Featherstone checked him out.

"Are you going back to the reservation Phil? I wonder if you could stop by the Double-B ranch and see if Leah is there. You'd pass her on the way back to town if she is on her way here so it wouldn't be a waste of your time. I'm a little worried that she hasn't returned from her ride with Amanda."

Philip said he would be glad to. Besides it would give him an excuse to say hello to Amanda. He had seen her only once since the barbecue and wanted to invite her to visit the reservation. He rode north toward the Double-B. The last rays of sunlight were on the horizon and stars were bright in the sky. He reached the Double-B. The steward answered the door. Philip could hear Braddock and Sir Charles discussing business in the parlor. Someone was playing piano. He asked to see Amanda rather than disturb the others. She came into the hall.

"Sorry to show up like this uninvited. But Mr. Featherstone is concerned that Leah has not returned home. Is she with you Amanda?"

Her welcoming smile faded.

"Oh, it's good to see you Philip. No, I haven't seen her all day. I told her yesterday that I couldn't go riding today and would come to town tomorrow to see her. This is alarming. Maybe she went on her own and hasn't returned."

"Do you have any idea where she might be?"

"It's possible she rode to our secret place. Where we go when we ride together. I hope she hasn't had an accident. Maybe we should go there."

She was suddenly worried and impulsively touched his arm.

"I'd be glad to go with you now. The sooner the better. I'll just change and be right out."

Amanda ran upstairs. He went onto the porch and after several minutes Amanda returned in her riding skirt and jacket. The night was cooler and the stars now filled the sky with brilliant chunks of light. Amanda went to the stable and led out her mare, Annabelle. With quick expert moves she saddled the horse. They were on their way in five minutes. Amanda was now entirely focused on getting to the secret place. Despite the darkness and the unvaried terrain, she had the instincts of an expert horsewoman and a strong sense of direction and time developed over many years riding in India and Egypt. They reached the river and stayed on the north bank, the reservation side. Philip admired her determination. They trotted, making good time, able to see reasonably well in the quarter moonlight.

"I believe that is the grove up ahead."

Amanda heeled Annabelle into a canter. Her anxiety increased as she approached the grove. Philip rode up behind her as she dismounted and ran toward the trees. He followed, lighting a small pitch torch that finally caught fire and projected dancing light and shadows as they entered the grove. He nearly ran into her as Amanda suddenly stopped. She gasped.

"Oh no!"

Her voice choked. She stood for a moment and then ran to the base of the large cottonwood that occupied the center position in the grove. Philip could finally see Leah, her body lying still as ivory at the base of the tree. Amanda had reached her and was kneeling, holding Leah's head in her arms, moaning, crying, deeper than grief, deeper than sorrow, a sorrow greater for the sweetness love and care in her voice.

"No, no, no, no...."

Amanda kept repeating like a musical phrase, cradling and rocking the dead girl's head and shoulders in her arms, kissing her hair, tears pouring down her cheeks.

"Oh my dear love, my dear love, my dear Leah..."

Amanda's sorrow and love and loss were so beautiful that Philip burst into tears. Her sorrow might have been for all the women who ever suffered pain and death, for all the daily beauty of the world that had been destroyed by envy, lust, and greed. But it was simply for Leah, for her loving beautiful friend, for her shy complicit smile when they first swam together, for her tender eager uncertain look as she presented Amanda with the dress she had sewn for her, for the grateful spontaneous kiss she gave Amanda when Amanda put the silver and turquoise necklace around her neck, for the graceful motion of her hands and body as she walked into the river, for the music of her gentle voice through all the hours they had spent together under the trees, under the sun, for the beautiful memory of Leah. Amanda grew quiet. Philip came up to her and gently pulled her away from Leah. He helped her to her feet and held her in his arms. She cried quietly as he smelled the lovely scent of her hair. His heart surged with love for this wonderful loving girl, as he pledged himself to serve, honor, love and protect her.

For two weeks after Leah's death, Amanda went out very little. The shock took time to heal. Philip rode to the ranch every day to enquire after her. She would come out onto the porch, they would say hello, then stand together for a while saying nothing. His presence comforted her. She felt especially alone since everyone in her entourage found the attachment to Leah unaccountable and her grief awkward. The funeral was very simple. Amanda was the only one from the eastern colony to attend. Melinda was there along with the other bar girls, Featherstone, Westmoreland, Philip. Melinda cried for Leah, a gentle lovely girl who always treated her politely and seemed so grateful for the flattering comments Melinda made about her appearance. *'What a lovely dress you have on Leah'* she would say. Leah had taken particular pride in her new necklace and Melinda had remarked on it the week before her murder. Melinda was not about to let this murder go unpunished.

She didn't know how, but she knew somehow, she would see the killer punished.

Philip invited Amanda to ride out to the reservation, and she agreed to go the following day. They headed north along the main road, then rode cross country for about five miles. The sage broom and grass were waving in the light breeze and the puffy clouds leisurely drifted eastward under a blue heaven. The rich heady perfume of thick clover, hay, and bursting new vegetation almost made them swoon. At one point Amanda laughed with sheer delight as they rode along, the first she had laughed since finding Leah.

Over the next few weeks, they rode out regularly, three or four times a week, exploring the river and visiting the reservation. Philip told her about Indian customs, life, desperate situation, unpromising future, the constant struggle to protect them from incursions, to guarantee their treaty rights. He introduced her to the Chiefs, who stoically nodded. The Indian women were shy and evasive, but they seemed to trust this kindly looking white woman. The children were more impulsive, even smiling back before running off. The array of teepees extended for hundreds of yards was impressive. The braves looked menacing and cruel. But she thought of them more as eagles and wolves or mountain lions, not hostile or evil, just naturally adapted to predation and having the brilliant predatory beauty of raptors.

He and Amanda occasionally picnicked in the small clusters of trees along the riverbank to find relief from the blazing afternoon sun. For a long time, she could not face returning to Leah's secret place. Then one day she felt it would bring her closer to her departed friend. However horrible her death, Amanda began to think of the grove as a sacred place holding the memory of their closeness and love. She and Philip returned there, and Amanda felt a strange peace, as if Leah were present protecting her with her love and caring. They returned regularly after that, picnicking and talking through the afternoons. Philip told her about his family in Philadelphia, his schools and aspirations, his first visit west in 1871 before leaving for Philips-Exeter Academy in Massachusetts. His return visits over the years in school and at Haverford College. His deep Quaker convictions of nonviolence and peacemaking. His shock at the treatment of Indians and his growing understanding of their way of life. Amanda told him of her years living in India and Egypt, her awe of her father, so handsome, brave and loving to her. She told him how the Indian people are so interesting, especially the women, with their quiet grace and intelligent eyes. Her best friend in Khalamphur was an Indian girl attending the English School.

Philip and Amanda became close friends as only quiet honest exchange of feelings and life experiences could do. They hardly noticed the time, and often returned to the Double-B ranch later than planned, creating some speculation as to what exactly they were up to and whether their independent meandering was wise. But Sir Charles was of the opinion that Amanda, now twenty years old, could take care of herself, and his hands were sufficiently occupied with Ariadne. Besides, Amanda had a life competence that provided well enough for her needs, present and prospective, and was in all respects a very sensible and capable girl needing little supervision from him. The others were so distracted by their own situations that Amanda hardly entered their thoughts.

The weeks of riding and talking restored Amanda's spirits, closed the wound of her loss, even if the experience would forever leave a scar. She smiled at Philip's earnest musings over life and death, as well as his sudden surprising wit. He adored her with all his soul, but refrained from saying or doing anything that might make her feel awkward or embarrassed. He would go on forever like this if he could, seeing her as often as possible, the sun, light and warmth of his life.

One afternoon they sat lazily talking, enjoying the balmy day, feeling drowsy from the picnic and unwilling to leave. A hundred miles west and out of their sight a dark line formed along the entire western rim of the horizon, barely perceptible at first, then rising, a ribbon of smoky grey and dense black. They didn't notice the faint intermittent stirrings of air, the falling silent of birds, so absorbed were they in the day and their thoughts. The black clouds now stood higher in the sky, whirls of smoky grey fingering into the still brilliant blue. The horizon edge was now entirely black, forked time to time by lightening, but so far away that the sound of thunder was barely audible to them.

Amanda was first to notice the new steady draft, not strong but seeming to gain strength and definite direction, becoming notably cooler. *"Feels like a storm coming Amanda. We'd better get going."* They packed up the picnic basket and walked out of the cluster of trees to the top of the hill. By now the storm had risen in black churning clouds to take up half of the horizon in a band a thousand miles wide below a perfectly clear and brilliant sky.

Lightening cracked along the horizon, smoky grey and brown columns streamed upward and downward before the black mass of the moving storm. The wind was now steady and perceptibly cooler, as the churning black wall rose ever higher in its approach. Lightening dashed across the far distance, throwing shards of blinding light into the utter darkness. Cottonwoods and willows whipped and bowed in the ever-stronger wind, then seemed to stagger under the stream of rain that broke over them, the plains grass flattening under the whip of wind-driven rain. Soon the sky was filled with a tidal wave of water, lightening, blackness, thunder, screaming wind lashing the treetops and whipping streams of water across the air. The first wash of rain reached them. As the black mass moved overhead, wind pressed Amanda's skirt against her as she held her face upward into the rain. Philip looked at Amanda and then at the storm, the steady wind-driven rain whipping his face. Lightening stabbed through the blackness forming cliffs of blinding light as caverns of deafening sound shook the earth.

The avalanche of rain was now constant, like a blanket thrown over them to protect them from the terrifying explosion of light and sound that surrounded them. They stood soaked with rain, eyes lifted to the sky. They glanced at each other then began to laugh, at first delightedly, then totally, uncontrollably, joyfully, cosmically as the wind-driven water washed and caressed them, as the lightening threw branches of searing white light around them, as the deafening thunder shook their trembling bodies and shattering earth, both feeling, just at that moment, that God, like a ray of sun in the darkest night, reached down, smiling, to hold them in his blazing hands.

Father Allen Montescue returned from the VanDuesen ranch later than expected and in a more unsettled state of mind than he would wish, the latter perhaps aggravated by more wine than he should have drunk and certainly more food than he should have eaten. Little Fox, his Indian houseboy, had gone to bed. The cook and maid lived just out of town and the parsonage was otherwise unoccupied.

Montescue entered the parlor and lit an oil lamp. He thought he might read a bit but couldn't concentrate. He sorted the mail on the end table of the sofa and opened a few letters with a letter opener. One from his sister in Rhode Island, her family well, but the youngest son is a bit of a rogue and problem at school. Montescue poured some sherry and just sat in his easy chair. The elegant surroundings no longer assuaged his sense of loneliness and frustration at spending nearly five months of the year in the wilds of Colorado. The first two years were bearable, but this year, the third, began to get him down. He had lost his belief long ago, if he ever truly had any. The ease and social advantages of his calling were adequate compensation in New York, where rich parishioners included him in their guest lists and where he presided over marriages, Christenings, burials, offering in resonant vocal form the soothing and sometimes rather preposterous texts appropriate to each occasion provided by the central administration of the church. The Persian rugs, Victorian furniture, Tiffany lamps and other paraphernalia he brought west to furnish his residence now seemed only to underscore his isolation, more a reminder of better times and places than a consolation in the new. New York offered other advantages as well, one of which was anonymity, a decided advantage for one so publicly constrained to observe conventions to the uttermost. He was in fact slightly drunk tonight, more than usually restless. He poured another sherry and leafed through an *Atlantic* magazine. He felt lonely, self-pity, a sense of wanting to break out of the constraints of his position. He reached for his glass and toppled it onto the rug. Annoyed, he rang the bell next to the lamp to summon the houseboy.

Little Fox was a Sioux boy placed with the parsonage to serve the pastor during his residence. Off season he returned to the reservation. The intent was teach him English so he could serve the tribe as an interpreter. Little Fox entered the parlor. He was fifteen-years old, with smooth light brown skin, slanted light-brown eyes, and high cheekbones. The light of the oil lamp outlined his body under the thin nightshirt, slender waist, well-proportioned almost girl-like form, hardly the image of the wild savage commonly understood back east. He was very mild in manner and hardly ever spoke.

"Little Fox, would you clean up this spill?"

The boy nodded, left the room for a moment, and returned with a cloth. He bent over and started mopping up the spilled sherry. Montescue felt sleepy and somewhat dizzy. The line of the boy's thigh showed through the nightshirt. Montescue looked at his smooth neck, the straight black hair reaching his shoulders, the soft curl of his ear, and the smooth round shape of his firm young buttocks. He felt a surge of desire work itself under his drowsiness. He wasn't thinking clearly if at all. The smooth lean body began to absorb what attention he could bring to bear, driven by a now urgent desire to touch and hold the boy. He moved closer, put his arms around the boy's waist and his lips to his neck. The boy turned with a panicked uncomprehending look.

"You are very beautiful Little Fox."

Montescue mumbled in a slurred voice curdled with desire. He pulled up the nightshirt and felt for the boy's penis, kissing the boy's arm and chest. Little Fox began to pull away and Montescue with mounting desperation fastened his grip, moving his mouth over the boy's body. The boy couldn't overpower the large white man, as he flailed his arms and nearly knocked over the oil lamp.

Montescue lost any rational control or awareness of what he was doing, so entirely consumed by months of agonizing loneliness, unrelieved desire, and self- pity. He freed his penis and turning the boy forcefully around he moved it between his buttocks. The boy struggled more violently and Montescue held him even harder, breathing heavily, gasping.

"You are so beautiful, you are so beautiful...."

Little Fox's hand moved against the table and grabbed the letter opener. He wrenched himself around to face Montescue and then with an underhand thrust drove the knife into the Priest's stomach. Montescue cried out and the boy in desperate fear drove the knife again and again into Montescue until he stopped screaming and released his grip. Montescue fell to his knees as the boy retreated in terror backward toward the front door, his eyes held to the last by the horror of streams of blood, the amazed quizzical pleading look on the face of the older man doubled up in the final moments of life.

"Found him dead---knifed in the belly."

Owen Bancroft, mayor and spokesman for the dude ranchers who made Del Norte whatever it could be said to be, spoke with lurid relish about the sensational murder of Father Allen Montescue. Sheriff Westmorland had been called at six that morning by the housekeeper who found the body. She was too hysterical to do more than drag the Sheriff out to the parsonage. Westmoreland looked at Bancroft with large blue eyes, deceptively innocent, like some child newly surprised by the infinite variety of human malfeasance.

"Who would do such a thing?"

Bancroft was incredulous that anyone would harm much less kill Father Montescue.

"Hard to figure. Religious man might have lots of enemies."

Westmoreland liked to quietly contradict commonly held assumptions. Bancroft was so absorbed by the gruesomeness of the crime he missed the Sheriff's irony.

"The Indian boy that worked for him seems to have disappeared. Guess he's our prime suspect until we know otherwise. I suppose you'll have to go to track him down on the reservation."

Westmoreland resented this overweight over-rich dude rancher from New York prescribing procedures. But the pay was good and a ride to the reservation would be a mere formality to keep his customers happy. The Indians wouldn't tell him where the boy is if they knew.

"Of course, it might have been a drifter. Almost impossible to catch that kind."

Westmorland threw out that suggestion as an alternative.

"It's terrible. Absolutely terrible. If there's anything we can do be sure to let us know."

Westmoreland smiled as appreciatively as personal contempt modified by political savvy allowed. The likelihood of Bancroft being of help under any circumstances hardly bore considering.

"Much obliged. Well, I'd better be going to the reservation to check the boy's whereabouts."

Leaving Bancroft with an agenda would reassure the gentry of his diligence in the matter for the time being. He could foresee daily inquiries as to how the case was progressing and was already arranging in his mind a series of mildly hopeful leads that would put them off so long as possible.

The horse had transformed the Plains Indian from a scratch farmer and grounded hunter into a sky god riding freely into the wind, hunting buffalo and soaring above an endless range like cumulous clouds and forked lightning. Of these centaur warriors, the greatest was Crazy Horse. For years no man took his photo or saw him up close. He attended no powwow with the white man, signed no treaties, left no trace. Yet he was the spiritual leader of the Plains Indians in the 1870's, leading their councils and moving from encampment to encampment to organize resistance to the white devils. He led the battle of Little Big Horn, riding in circles, wearing his war bonnet, firing his rifle with deadly effect, and for him was reserved the kill of General Custer. After the battle he moved to Montana and then to Canada, establishing routes of retreat for the Sioux as they faced defeat after defeat, himself killed in the course of a visit to an Army fort to arrange a cease fire in 1876.

By 1882, the war was lost and the tribes were trapped and dispirited on the reservations left them by treaty. James Westmoreland rode into the Sioux camp and approached the circle of Chiefs in front of a large teepee. They stood expressionless as Westmoreland raised his right hand in greeting. Chief Lightening Before Rain lifted his hand in reply. He motioned to the teepee and they all went inside, the Chiefs resuming a circle, sat cross legged. Chief Lightening Before Rain lit a peace pipe, then passed it to his left. Each Chief took a puff. It came round to Westmoreland. He took a puff and passed it on. Nothing was said. Westmoreland and Chief Lightening Before Rain sat looking at each other. Westmoreland nodded. The Chiefs knew why he came. Westmoreland knew they knew. He would wait until they were ready to tell him whatever they were going to tell him. He might get the truth, he might get nothing. He didn't care either way.

Chief Lightening Before Rain

After years in the west, he had come to know the Indians. He didn't love them, he didn't hate them. He respected them. They were fighters, they were losing, they were proud in defeat. They had a sense of personal honor, despite the shocking atrocities they were capable of. He waited, observing the faces in the circle around him. They resembled the faces he had seen at battle conferences in the South late in the Civil War. Creased, tired, driven, hopelessness not even a factor, honor being the last motive when all reasonable advantage or prospect was gone. He used to think the Indian names were absurd. Lightening Before Rain, Little Fox, Little Bear. He now had respect for, if not understanding of, these strange people, their mystical character. But mostly, their sense of honor, unwilling to quit, trying to the last to remain unbroken in the face of unmitigated disaster and the ruin of their way of life, caged in tents and reservations, having lost the wild free-roaming life they led in pursuit of the buffalo over the Great Plains.

Westmoreland saw the impossibility of that life continuing in the face of mass migration to the West. Farms and ranches brought property, ownership, and economic management to the land that Indians considered sacred and a gift, a loan, not a possession. The idea of property, of destroying the land to obtain riches, wealth they would not have considered to be wealth, was alien to them. A smattering of eagle feathers and buffalo hides hardly matched the trainloads of cattle, wheat, logs, copper, gold dust and people that moved along the steel rails that now and forever severed the Great Plains into economic regions. The Chiefs muttered a few words, and signed agreement. Westmoreland looked at Lightening Before Rain as he began signing.

Westmoreland had acquired a rudimentary knowledge of Indian sign language, mostly from Philip Cadwallader. The Chief described Montescue as a holy man. He signed Little Fox. Then signed woman. Then seizing with both hands. A sign for sexual union between male and female. Then a sign for knife and stabbing. Then a sign for flight. Westmoreland for a moment thought he had been mistaken, misinterpreted. He signed a question. The Chief repeated the sequence, expressionless. Westmoreland finally understood. He looked at the Chief for a long moment. The other Chiefs looked at Westmoreland.

Westmoreland had of course heard of such propensity. The military was not without such examples. But it was encountered so rarely that he had not thought of that as an explanation until this very moment. He signed that he understood. He signed a boy and urgent flight. He signed that the matter was closed for him. He then got up, as the Chiefs stood. They signed peace and farewell. Westmoreland walked out of the tent, mounted, waved goodbye and rode back to Del Norte.

Nearly every day Ariadne went to the stables. She and Brandon had fallen so deeply in love that for the first week they did nothing but make urgent love in the warm straw at the back of the stalls, tender, violent, overpowering. After a week or so they went riding along the river, finding a cluster of cottonwoods. They went swimming first. Sheltered by the overhanging branches of the cottonwoods they would lie on a blanket, make love, sleep in each other's arms. Ariadne was so hungry for him she made him make love to her until he could no longer. She seemed not to care about anything but the passion they shared and the growing love that seemed to underlie the passion. Brandon was as much in love with her as she was with him. After nearly six weeks had passed, Ariadne realized she was pregnant. She did not feel alarmed, just surprised, as if this outcome were not the obvious outcome of their love making. She told Brandon, and he, perhaps beyond what she expected, was delighted, told her they should marry immediately and that he would arrange it. She approached Sir Charles one morning privately.

"Father, I want to marry right away."

Sir Charles, preoccupied with the much prolonged trip due to complications in arranging access to copper resources on the Indian reservation, appeared not to understand.

"Well of course, when we get back to England Lord Basil will likely want to fix the date. After all, you have been putting it off, not he."

"I don't mean Basil. I want to marry Brandon Evans, the ranch manager. I'm pregnant."

Sir Charles, after years of experience in the world, and endowed with exceptional intellectual powers, required only a moment to calculate the possible antecedents to such a request. Lacking exact details or even a clear sense of the time in which a relationship might have been consummated, he nonetheless understood intuitively the situation and had already begun reviewing the possible means by which the situation might be saved.

"Ariadne, get this perfectly clear. You may do whatever you want. But if you marry some cowboy, you will never receive a farthing from me. You may choose to live in a tent on the prairie and raise a brood, but you will do it alone, excepting your Brandon, I assume."

She bristled at the contempt with which he referred to Brandon. He continued.

"There is another possibility. You might, if you have not already, seduce Basil, as soon as possible. He then will be honor bound to cover the blessed event as promptly as possible. It may even add a dash of pepper to his

reputation to show the world how red-blooded he is. A premature birth among aristocrats would mean little and since you were engaged before leaving England, it would be blamed on the licentious atmosphere of the American Wild West."

He stopped to examine how she was taking this proposal. Her face reddened.

"Basil is a fairy. I've already tried to seduce him and all he did was to say he would do nothing to betray the trust you placed in him!"

Sir Charles frowned at this, now unfortunate, news. Less moral fiber and more impetuosity in Basil would have been welcome.

"You realize you would be giving up all the elegance, power, property that comes with the title Lady Pomeroy. Think about that. Whatever enthusiasm led to your unfortunate condition may pall over years of living in a tent, scrubbing clothes and cooking bacon over a hot iron stove in the middle of this godforsaken wilderness. I say this only for your own good. Think of the long run. And there ARE ways to deal with the situation."

Sir Charles suggested she meditate on what he had said and promptly left her to meet with Braddock. Ariadne was restless for several days, sending a message to Brandon that she was unwell and would resume riding when she felt better. At night she turned in her sleep, tormented by the divided claims of wealth and position versus the rich-blooded passion of her lover Brandon. She began to look distracted and really unwell. Amanda asked what the matter was. Ariadne said it was just a cold.

Rosalinda a Mexican maid was quietly tidying up her room. She spoke a little English which accounted for her comparatively high status as a house servant. Ariadne spoke to her.

"Rosalinda, could I ask you a very confidential question?"

Rosalinda smiled quizzically, understanding the words but having no idea what she could know that such a beautiful White women would ask her about.

"I need a doctor. A baby doctor. Do you understand?"

Rosalinda crossed herself.

"Please Rosalinda. You or someone you know in town must know of one. Maybe there is a woman who does such things."

Rosalinda looked frightened.

"Senorita, I cannot do this."

"Please. I need someone soon."

It took some time before Rosalinda agreed to find out if there was anyone able to deal with Ariadne's condition, which she had eventually described to Rosalinda much to her surprise and shock. Two days later she told Ariadne that there was a doctor in town who might be able to help her. She could see him the next day around noon at his residence on the outskirts of town. Ariadne persuaded Rosalinda to accompany her. They agreed to meet a mile from the ranch on the road to town. Ariadne encountered Brandon at the stable, where he had saddled her mare. She told him she would come to see him later in the week as he handed her the reins.

"You don't look well Ariadne. Is there anything I can do? Has your father agreed to our marriage?"

She smiled and rode off. Rosalinda was waiting on the road to town and Ariadne had her mount behind her. They reached the shack where the putative doctor resided. A man of about fifty came to the door, grizzled, unkempt, intelligent looking but obviously having seen better days. Whether because of whisky, disappointment, injury, or illness, his watery red eyes looked bleakly at Ariadne, but even his reduced state of expectation was stirred by the presence of this beautiful, troubled girl, who had taken it upon herself to seek an abortion without the least concern for the possible serious medical consequences. She went inside and explained the situation.

"Bad business as you know. I can do it but it is illegal and could get us into big trouble. I need $500 so I can leave Del Norte and avoid any legal complications."

He looked at her, wondering if he had hit too low a price.

"I'll pay. What do I have to do."

"It will take about an hour. You have to rest several hours afterward before you can return home. I will need the help of your maid. You will have to ride in a carriage. This will be difficult to bring off without arousing suspicions."

"I'll take care of the carriage. When can we proceed?"

"As far as I'm concerned, anytime. But I'll need the money before we start."

"You'll have it. What about day after tomorrow?"

Ariadne returned to the ranch relieved that her inconvenient condition might soon be resolved. The matter of $500 was settled by asking Lord Basil to advance the amount for unspecified reasons. Because he felt at a disadvantage in other respects, his ability to provide money restored some of his damaged self-esteem and to some extent placed Ariadne under his power again reaffirming his contextual advantages that might offset his deficient personal ones.

The next day she drove a small carriage to the doctor's shack, Rosalinda saying hail Mary's en route. The doctor set up a long table with basins. Water boiled on the iron wood stove some surgical instruments lay on a platter next to the table. An oil lamp hung over the table and two others in the room were lit. In the dark beyond the table were a rumpled bed, a table for meals, and two chairs.

He told Ariadne to remove her skirt and underclothes. She could keep her clothes on above the waist. He asked her to lie on the long table and gave her enough morphine tablets to put her to sleep. The morphine took effect, and she dozed off sufficiently that he could proceed. There was a bottle of whisky nearby. He poured some into a basin and began the operation. It took about fifteen minutes. When it was over, he told Rosalinda to remain with Ariadne until she awakened. Rosalinda was crying. The doctor washed his hands, rolled down his sleeves and put on his coat. A valise was by the door. He took the valise and opened the door.

"Remember, just let her sleep. When she wakes up, wait until she feels well enough to move, then take her home."

He shut the door and headed for town. If he ran he could just make the two o'clock eastbound train.

Rosalinda waited for two hours. Ariadne then began to moan, gradually regaining consciousness as the morphine wore off. She felt a sharp pain. She didn't feel she could move. She lay there for another hour. Then she decided she better get back to the ranch. Rosalinda helped her to her feet, got her skirt on, and they walked to the carriage. Ariadne could barely stand the pain on the way home, the carriage jolts shooting through her like brands of fire. They got to the ranch. Rosalinda brought her in the back way and got her to her room. She undressed her and put her to bed, terrified at how pale and distracted Ariadne looked. Once in bed, Ariadne went right to sleep. Rosalinda left the room and ran downstairs, not knowing what to do next.

By late afternoon, Amanda had returned home from her ride with Philip. The others had been lunching at a neighboring ranch and got back about nine o'clock, the notions of lunch being very elastic among the eastern colony. Amanda was first to notice Ariadne was feverish. She ordered compresses and tried to talk to her, but she was delirious. Amanda asked if there was a doctor anywhere who could be called. One of the ranch owners was a doctor and served the colony in emergencies. He was called and arrived around midnight.

By then Ariadne was in severe fever. The doctor was perplexed by possible causes, at first assuming it might be a typhoid infection. He asked Amanda's assistance in examining Ariadne. When he discovered the cause, he blenched, looking at Amanda in horror.

"My God!"

He stood for a moment, the shock taking some interval to pass before he could resume a medical assessment of the chances for Ariadne's recovery.

"Keep her warm, despite the fever. There is nothing we can do but wait. She has lost blood. She is weakened from this horrible act, but she is

young and there is a remote chance she can fight off the infection. I will say nothing of this. I trust you will keep it to yourself as well."

He looked kindly at Amanda and left the room. The diagnosis of typhoid fever passed immediately to the entire colony. Ariadne lingered for four days. Sometimes it seemed that the fever would abate, then it resumed with greater force. She became very pale and thin. Toward the end she was entirely delirious, when she was conscious. Nothing she said was understood, but it seemed she was calling for something or someone. Brandon heard of the illness and Rosalinda admitted him by the back way. He cried helplessly beside her bed for an hour, before Rosalinda asked him to leave. He came several times, looking desperate and afraid, as he saw the love of his life, the center of his being wasting away before him.

Lord Basil was equally diligent in his visits to her bedside, often in company with Sir Charles and Braddock. Lord Basil also came at intervals on his own, as if acquitting himself of duties incurred as prospective spouse. As death approached, he felt some tenderness for her, but that was fleeting. More often he felt relief, as if a great burden were about to be removed from his life. Lord Basil was accomplished at the outward forms of grief. The absence of deep feeling made him especially able to console Sir Charles, who was terribly shaken by Ariadne's death. Uninformed of the true cause, he felt no guilt at his suggestion that the child might be disposed of. The loss of his only child, the wild daughter he had for so many years dispatched to boarding schools while he pursued financial schemes, now seemed deeply important.

Melinda stood on the wooden porch outside the saloon. The late afternoon was hot, sultry. The first scent of moist cool air and the cloudburst to come were just perceptible. A few ladies had completed errands at the general store and were hurrying home. Mrs. Frost, wife of the Baptist minister, ignored Melinda's greeting. Despite his Hell and brimstone approach to salvation, poor Revered Emmanuel Frost had a weakness for whisky. His occasional binges were forgiven as simply God's way of testing his soul and giving him the human weakness that actually increased his authority with the congregation. Everyone liked old 'fire and brimstone', first for putting on a real show, unlike the bloodless Montescue, and second for making getting up on Sunday morning something of an event.

Several men, part of a caravan headed for Oregon, were buying provisions at the general store. Potshot talked to one of the women with them, a young girl with a baby in her arms. She looked skeptical. He appeared to be showing her something, but Melinda couldn't see what it was and was not particularly interested. The mellow feel of storm air building felt good, and she dreamily relaxed.

Suddenly something caught her eye as Potshot turned halfway in her direction, a glint of silver and turquoise in the last rays of the setting sun. She felt a surge of uneasiness, searching for why this should strike her so oddly. She tried to get a better look at what Potshot was showing the young mother. She saw it was some kind of necklace or bracelet. Then, as if hit in the stomach, she gasped. She remembered Leah Featherstone wore a silver and turquoise necklace. Melinda couldn't take her eyes off Potshot. The young mother apparently found the price too high or wasn't particularly interested in acquiring something so entirely decorative. Potshot gave up and wandered down the street. Melinda stared after him trying to piece together the implications of what she had seen. Eventually she went inside and upstairs to her room to take a nap.

Around nine o'clock Potshot came into the saloon. By now it was busy, cowboys, drifters, soldiers on leave, a few local residents, and Rain Cloud at the end of the bar hungrily downing whatever drink he could cadge from the others. Allison played piano. Cowboys danced with two Indian girls who provided low-cost favors. Potshot ordered two whiskeys. Somehow it all fell into place without Melinda having to actually formulate it in her mind. She moved over to Potshot at the bar and said:

"Buy me a drink?"

He looked surprised, even frightened at first. Then his face deformed into a stubble smile and knowing look.

"Why sure. Barkeep, one more for the little lady."

She forced a bleak smile and said:

"Champagne, Gabe. This guy knows how to treat a girl right."

She moved a little closer to Potshot. He was gaining courage from the whisky and the apparent turnaround in Melinda's attitude toward him. He started talking about moving to California, about what a lot of money he could make, and by implication, how much smarter he was than most of the people who had preceded him in that direction. By ten o'clock, Potshot was drunk, had spent $40 on Champagne, and was making lustful suggestions to Melinda. She laughed.

"How much you got?"

He tried $20 but she laughed harder, and he tried $40.

"I'll think about it."

She started to move to another part of the saloon. He grabbed her arm and in a husky voice said:

"Sixty bucks. That's all I got."

She looked at him carefully and nodded.

"Follow me upstairs after a couple of minutes."

Melinda turned toward the back end of the saloon, swiveling her hips as she walked to the stairs and headed upstairs to her room. Once in her room she had no definite idea what to do next. The noise in the saloon was now quite deafening--singing, shouting, thumping boots on the thin pinewood floor. Every now and then a cowboy would go outside and shoot off a few rounds in sheer exuberance. Westmoreland didn't enforce the public silence laws until after midnight on Saturdays, and then only because churchgoers complained.

Potshot stumbled down the dark hallway toward the light visible under the door. He turned the knob without knocking and walked in. The large bed took up most of the room, a dresser near the window, a bowl and towels opposite the door, a table with a lit oil lamp, and a chandelier with four candles. Melinda stood near the window. Potshot grinned as lasciviously as three bottles of champagne would allow. She said:

"Get undressed and into bed."

Like a schoolboy under orders, he unbuckled his gun belt and unbuttoned his shirt. She told him to put the guns on the chair near the end of the bed. He sat on the bed and took off his boots, then unbuttoned his pants and pulled them off. He lay back on the bed nude and looked at her. He was erect and looked like some macabre vision of the banality of sensual desire. Melinda pulled her blouse from her skirt and pulled it over her head, swaying her breasts at him. She pulled down her skirt and began swaying her hips. She never wore underclothes and her body warmed suggestively in the dim light of the oil lamp.

"Hot damn!"

That seemed to be all he could find to say as he ogled her cocoa brown body.

"You like chocolate candy, big boy?"

She moved toward the chair.

"You got a big stick for mama!"

He laughed. She picked up his gun belt and removed the revolver.

"What a big gun you got honey."

He misunderstood the reference and grinned harder. She opened the cartridge chamber and saw it was full, then clicked it back into place.

"You like us colored girls, right? Niggers, Indians, Mexicans, you name it, huh?"

She smiled but her voice was hard. He saw the smile, didn't hear the change in tone.

"Hot damn! You are the most gorgeous pussy I ever saw. Come over here quick."

She lost her smile, but he wasn't following her face that closely.

"What about Leah? You like her pussy too?"

She hissed the words, but resumed the set smile.

"I don't know no Leah."

He turned suspicious. He covered his penis which had succumbed to gravity.

"Oh yeah, you know Leah, big boy. I saw you holding her necklace. It was a present from her friend and she thought it was wonderful. But you took it from her, you took everything from her."

She let the anger rise in her voice, move to her eyes, as she raised the revolver point blank at him. The crowd downstairs acted with perfect timing, several on the street shooting their revolvers, others in the saloon dancing and singing wildly. All desire drained from Potshot's face. Overwhelming dread entered his eyes, his body shaking.

"Hey, wait, you got it all wrong. I never touched her. I got that necklace from a guy who lost at cards and...."

He tried smiling insinuatingly, offering plausible excuses for having the necklace, trying anything to move the barrel of that gun in any direction but his. He didn't finish the sentence as the first bullet crashed through his clavicle. The second went into his stomach. The third through his forehead. Melinda let the gun drop, out of sheer exhaustion. Blood was all over the bed. She stood for a moment, then put on her clothes. She found a small trunk, packed a few valuables and put her money in her handbag. She had $800, enough to start a new life in California. Westmoreland would go through the motions, but she knew he wouldn't pursue her, and no arm of the law was long enough to find her once she reached San Francisco.

She stepped into the hall and went down the back stairs. The night was cooling, and the first drops of rain began to fall. She lifted her face to the sky, breathing deeply. The westbound train was due in fifteen minutes. No one would check her room until morning. Certainly, Gabe would not bother her until well after things slowed down in the saloon. She hated to leave him with the mess, but he would understand. She headed for the station and waited at the end of the platform. Ten passengers were waiting as well so she was less noticeable. She put her shawl over her head and held her face down. The train would get to Denver by four o'clock. She could get off in Denver and take a stage to Tucson, Arizona, or she could take the train west through Utah and on to California. If Westmoreland delayed wiring a description or perhaps not do so at all, she could get beyond any immediate risk of apprehension by Monday when the official apparatus of law enforcement, such as it was, might reach a threatening level of efficiency. Fortunately, States didn't waste much time tracking others' offenders and had few resources to do so.

The train pulled into the station. In ten minutes, it would load and depart. She waited until the last minute, then climbed into a Pullman car. The platform conductor cried *"All aboard"*. The train began to move, in billows of coal smoke and the whine of spinning wheels. No one came running to the platform, no one shouted *"Stop! Stop!"* The train left the station and headed into the moon-brightened dark of Coloado plains toward the black snow-capped sawteeth of the Rocky Mountains.

Following the trip to the minefields and the report from the mining engineers, Braddock and Sir Charles had been perplexed by their findings. The only major and feasibly exploitable deposits were within the Indian reservation, an endowment guaranteed by formal treaty between the United States and the Sioux nation. Any use or transfer of such land required the consent of the tribe. Their first approach was to offer royalties, which were rejected on principle. The land was, if not sacrosanct, at least somewhat 'holy' with gravesites and spiritual places. They then began exploring political routes, contacting Senators in particular who might arrange a modification in treaty terms, something on the order of the much later irreverent notion of J. Paul Getty that *'the meek shall inherit the earth, but not the mineral rights'*. Indians could have the surface assets, but the US retained control and rights of disposal of underlying mineral deposits. This argument met vigorous opposition, especially in New England where that region's proclivity toward sanctimonious posturing (so described by other regions) ensured adamant opposition to another betrayal by fork-tongued white men. Several weeks were expended on these inexpedient solutions. There remained one other.

Braddock and Sir Charles sent word they would like to meet with Colonel Drake at his convenience. Drake sent word that it was convenient for him to ride out to the Double-B ranch the following day. He arrived mid-morning. Braddock showed him into the library where Sir Charles was writing letters.

"Welcome Colonel. It was good of you to come. You know Sir Charles Winthrop I believe. Would you like a drink?"

Drake, sensing a test behind the offer, declined. He would lose stature if he accepted a drink in what appeared as a business not casual meeting, he would be placed at a moral disadvantage in a manner of speaking. Until he knew the precise nature of the business at hand, he would remain aloof, formal and uncommitted by any familiarity.

"We asked you here to discuss a proposition. Our discussion will begin and end here. Only you and I and Sir Charles will know what was said here. You may of course withdraw at anytime."

Drake smiled at the *la-de-da* preliminary. His ear for conspiracy led him to think this will be a very interesting morning, especially because he rightly intuited that they needed him much more than he needed them.

"I get the idea, go ahead."

"As you know Colonel, Sir Charles and I have invested in a mining venture. The project is under way and a number of test drills have been made. Our mining engineers have reported to us. Apparently significant deposits of copper and other valuable metals are located on the Sioux reservation. Under treaty they possess rights to those deposits. Am I clear so far?"

"I get the picture Braddock, you would like to remove the Indians from the reservation and take over the mineral rights."

Sir Charles poured himself a brandy.

"We need some means to force the Indians out of the reservation while preserving a semblance of legality. Certainly, we must gain popular approval in order to muster political support. That's why we asked you here, Colonel."

Braddock assumed a more intimate and amiable demeanor, lowering his voice confidentially as he did so.

"Any ideas you may have would be much appreciated."

Drake laughed. Realizing that they were now at the disadvantage, he decided to have that drink.

"I think I will have a whisky after all. I see we are talking major larceny here, entirely inconsistent with the oath of an officer in the US Army. I will for the moment divest myself of that position and speak simply as one entrepreneur to another. You would like some pretext, possibly an armed incident between the Army and the Indians, that would excuse an attack on the reservation, constitute a violation that would invalidate the treaty, and force the Sioux to leave. Carefully coordinated with reports to Washington, the Congress and newspapers that would drum up outrage sufficient to overcome any effort to establish the truth of the situation. Under attack, the Sioux might decide to move north, possibly to Canada, leaving the reservation more or less open to your claims. Am I clear so far?"

Drake tossed the whisky down and laughed again at Braddock and Sir Charles. Both the latter relaxed, finding comfort in such agreeable and unmitigated insight into their immediate need. They began to like

Drake a great deal. The larger question of what might be required by Drake in return remained.

"Of course, you would be asking me to commit crimes under Federal law. I would be misusing the military forces under my command, deliberately inciting the Sioux, possibly starting another Indian war. When the inevitable investigation into the event occurs, I risk court martial and possible imprisonment. That's a lot to ask for a shot of whisky."

He laughed again and looked sharply at both men.

"Listen Colonel, we fully intend to reward you handsomely for whatever you may be able to do for us. We can for example offer you a twenty percent interest in the mining venture itself."

Drake smiled with just a trace of contempt that such a transparent ruse would be tried on him.

"My dear Braddock, for all I know that mining venture may be a worthless sham to gull investors and make you rich. I want a transfer out of here. I also want a substantial deposit of gold into my New York account, say $50,000. In return I can create an incident that will likely drive the Sioux from the reservation. You will have to drum up local anger against the Sioux. The murder of Montescue might be a good excuse. Following an armed incident, we need to be first with civil and Army reports. If the Indian agent gets ahead of us, the story may not play back east, and Congress will send out a committee instead of more troops."

Braddock took in the plan, nodded.

"I think we understand each other perfectly Colonel. We agree to your terms and will begin immediately the fund transfer and a campaign back East against the Sioux. Enough prominent financial and business people have ranches here to influence the people who count in Washington, including arranging your transfer."

"I say this calls for Champagne."

Sir Charles was much heartened by the undisguised larceny of his new partners. Braddock ordered Champagne while Drake downed another whisky.

Amanda and Philip reached the Sioux reservation by four o'clock. They rode into the encampment, squaws quietly busy near the tents, the tribal leaders standing erect, frowning, to welcome them. Philip conducted a routine review of the tribe's condition and compliance with the terms of the treaty, which included insuring that they received the supplies and subsidies promised them. Little was spoken, although occasionally Philip would say something in Oglala. The ritual inspection proceeded quickly.

He explained to Amanda the hierarchy of Chiefs, the role of women, the demeaning change in Plains Indian way of life caused by confinement to the reservation. The children looked shyly at her. She smiled and they ducked away, some smiled. She walked over to one, kneeled and held out her hand. The child smiled but ran to her mother. The women neither smiled nor appeared hostile. There was a pervasive sense of poverty, scarcity, and despair faced with resilience and pride.

Amanda and Philip moved around the teepees that extended over half a square mile, home to perhaps nine thousand Indians. No one bothered or cared to count them. Philip explained that buffalo had provided abundant food, clothing, shelter and prosperity and a spiritual life based on hunting and nomadic following the herds. Now the Indians were reduced to farming and hunting small game.

At first, they didn't particularly notice or feel alarmed by the shouting that began at the northern end of the encampment. Only after the first shots did Philip sense something was seriously wrong. The Indians had been disarmed, but for a few low caliber rifles needed for hunting. It was unlikely that they would be firing near the camp where game was practically nonexistent. The camp began to stir, women ran here and there, braves rushed toward the sound of firing, shouts adding to the confusion. The firing increased. Philip told Amanda to wait while he ran toward the source of the commotion. She said '*No*', she would go with him, and they both ran toward the edge of the camp. As they passed teepees, braves emerged with rifles and ran along beside them. The shooting, cries, shouts, and noise grew louder. Several soldiers held a squaw while one of them raped her. Another shot an Indian boy who screamed and tried to pull the soldier off his mother. Another group shot into the teepees, while one torched them. Ponies corralled in the center of the camp whinnied and bucked in wild fear. Several braves released their stay ropes, and the ponies ran wildly through the camp. Black acrid smoke from the burning buffalo hides filled the air, choking Philip and Amanda. They became separated. Confusion was total, squaws ran with children crying and screaming, braves rushed toward the soldiers with tomahawks, spears, some with rifles. Philip had no idea what he could do to stop the killing. He shouted in the soldiers' direction but could hardly hear himself above the melee. Several soldiers had been killed, but many more Indians were dead or wounded. He thought of Amanda and started back to where they had been separated.

Amanda gathered several women and children to lead them away from the slaughter. The smoke burned her eyes. The noise made it impossible to think, like walking through some Hell without exit. Three soldiers approached her group and began firing at the Indians. One of them grabbed Amanda and ripped off her dress. She screamed and hit him but he was too strong for her. Another half-drunk with whisky grinned:

"Nice white Indian loving pussy, we'll show you."

She kicked at him which made him laugh louder. He grabbed one of her ankles. Another soldier grabbed her other ankle and a third held her arms behind her. She fought as hard as she could, the soldiers enjoying her futile struggle. The first soldier called her '*Fucking bitch*' and started to move in on her. Philip ran up to him and pulled him back. The soldier turned, startled, as the others watched. He threw a punch at Philip that swung wide. Philip hit him solidly in the gut and he doubled up. The soldier reached for his holster, and Philip hit him with an undercut to the jaw. It stung his knuckles as the soldier began bleeding from the nose. The other soldiers reached for their revolvers. Philip reflexively pulled the first soldier to him as a shield and turning him, pulled the revolver from his holster. The other two were about to shoot Philip. He fired at one, then the other, shooting the first through the neck, the other in the chest. Blood spurted over Amanda, and the two soldiers dropped to the ground. The first soldier screamed:

"Oh my God, don't shoot me!"

Philip released his hold and the soldier crawled and then ran screaming off into the smoke. Philip ran up to Amanda who was crying hysterically.

"It's all right now Amanda. It's all right."

He covered her with her torn dress, lifted her, and carried her to one of the nearby teepees. The Indians had gained ground against the attackers as firing moved away from the center of the camp. Philip lay Amanda on a blanket. She regained composure, still sobbing but responding to his reassurances. He began to sob with the release of tension. She reached up to caress his face, to say everything will be all right, that there was nothing he could do, that he saved her life. They wept in each other's arms, as he said over and over and over..,

"Amanda, Amanda, Amanda...."

Braddock prepared a written report of the incident signed by Owen Bancroft, Mayor of Del Norte, on behalf of the entire community, and telegraphed it to Washington, Chicago, New York and Boston. In addition, he mobilized financial support for action against the Sioux over the next few days. Philip sent his own report of the incident to his office in Washington. Amanda informed Braddock and Sir Charles of what happened. She was outraged at the attack of the soldiers against the Indians and told Philip she would willingly testify to any official inquiry. Braddock considered it extraordinary luck that Philip had shot and killed two soldiers. Colonel Drake received a report of Philip's action the day after the incident and rode over to see Braddock, who was considering how to use this information.

"I see a number of ways to turn this to our advantage. First, the Indians were well armed with new rifles. That suggests that smugglers were making deliveries, and the Indian Agent could be accused of connivance. Whether or not that is true, and in this case, it is unlikely, he is the only white man authorized to inspect the reservation and ascertain compliance with the treaty, so the public will feel he should have known about the rifles."

Braddock nodded assent.

"In addition, he shot and killed two soldiers, who were allegedly attempting to rape your guest. I have no doubt that is true. However, if we can present our story first, we can say she just happened to be present, and the soldiers were trying to protect her."

Braddock poured two whiskies and offered one to Drake.

"I will issue a warrant for his arrest under military authority, charging treason and murder. If we place him under martial law, he will be at considerable disadvantage in getting his account of events believed. As to the soldier who survived and reported the killings, he will be more than happy to corroborate our explanation, since he has already lied about it and would face court martial and possible hanging if he admitted to the crime of rape against a white woman. I certainly will make him fully aware of this."

Braddock agreed. He could not directly participate in the scheme because he was still feigning support for Amanda's version of events. Sir Charles was another matter. He had not imagined that his niece would be involved so directly and violently in the incident he had connived at, and was shaken by the direct personal consequences of what he had been pleased to regard abstractly as a deal between the military and economic interests to advance the prosperity of both at the expense of the expendable natives. But the near rape of his niece combined with the loss of Ariadne inspired misgivings he would not otherwise have had.

Braddock decided not to tell Sir Charles of his agreement with Colonel Drake, and to continue his apparent outrage and support of Amanda's efforts to get out the truth. That day and the next he arranged for a false account following the lines laid out by Drake to be sent to key authorities, newspapers and economic interests back east, while Drake issued a military warrant and telegraphed the charges and explanation to Washington. The conspiracy worked swiftly, as members of Congress and the press spread their version and the formal charges against Philip.

Philip remained at the reservation following the attack. Amanda was unhurt but badly shaken and he left her with two squaws. He counted the casualties, the damage to the Indian camp, and conferred with the Chiefs. He told them he would prepare a report immediately condemning the soldiers for their attack and call on Washington to send a review commission to inquire into the incident.

He then returned to Amanda who was much recovered, and they rode back to the Double-B ranch. He reported to Braddock on what happened, and then rode to Del Norte to talk with Sheriff Westmoreland.

The Sheriff heard of the incident from Mayor Owen Bancroft, who reported with uncommon speed. The Mayor first telegraphed an account of the incident to Washington and other points east, then went to the Sheriff to complain about law enforcement in general and his failure to apprehend the murderer of Father Montescue in particular. Westmoreland was tempted to tell him what he knew about the murder but smiled gamely at the fat, rich little man, musing on the curious outcome of history that such a preposterous figure should be the beneficiary of so momentous an event as the Civil War. Bancroft had made his money supplying the Union soldiers with uniforms, money subsequently invested in railroad expansion. Philip entered Westmoreland's office, interrupting these musings.

"You've heard what happened? Drake attacked the reservation without provocation. I'm going to file a complete report to Washington."

Westmoreland had never seen him so angry.

"Worse yet, I shot two soldiers who were trying to rape Amanda Egerton. She's fine now, but I have to report that as well. Otherwise, Drake will probably accuse me of outright murder."

"You can lay money on it. Why don't you send your report as soon as possible. Our mayor already sent his version which blames the Sioux and makes the Army look like potted saints. I imagine Drake had it all written up a week ago."

He pat Philip on the shoulder as they moved toward the door. Westmoreland headed uptown toward the hotel. He was thinking over the likely sequence of the next several days. He most wanted to know what the Chiefs were up to. They had been attacked, and the fact that they had rifles contrary to treaty provisions meant that no matter what they claimed in their defense, they would be accused of conspiracy to rearm and resume the war. That they were acting in self-defense would be no excuse. He went upstairs and down the hallway to his room.

Philip wrote his report and sent it by pouch on the eleven o'clock train to Washington. He wrote a summary and telegraphed it as well. He requested an investigation into the conduct of Colonel Drake and the causes of the incident. He was not sanguine about the outcome. Although prejudice against the Indians had abated somewhat, no active sympathy had taken its place. For most Americans, a discreet gradual elimination of the tribes from potentially valuable farm and ranch lands was perfectly acceptable. Actions that were grossly unjust were immediately condemned but even those actions if they contributed to the removal of Indians from the path of settlers and progress were eventually forgotten.

Two days after the incident, Braddock hosted another community gathering, called ostensibly by Mayor Bancroft. The eastern colony was vocal and angry. The gallant defense by Army soldiers attacked while on routine patrols near the reservation was feelingly described by survivors. The description by one soldier was so embellished that Colonel Drake interrupted him on grounds of sparing the women present the gruesome description of scalping and cutting out of hearts.

For many reasons, Philip could not attend the gathering. For one, Drake had already charged him with murder and issued a warrant for his arrest. Amanda was present and listened in silence until the last soldier spoke. Then she stood up and insisted on giving her account of the incident. Despite protests from some in the colony, Braddock asked that she be allowed to speak. Amanda told of how she had visited the reservation with Philip Cadwallader, how they heard shooting, and how the soldiers attacked from the northern boundary of the camp. How three soldiers attempted to rape her and how Philip had to shoot two of them in self-defense and to protect her. She spoke quietly and intensely, without a trace of hysteria or anger that would otherwise have compromised the effect of her story. She said the Indians were behaving peaceably and had not provoked the attack and were probably victims of a plot to drive them off the reservation. She ended with a plea for justice and tolerance.

Silence followed, as everyone present felt the truth of her words, undermining the more welcome convenient and lurid accounts they had heard from the soldiers. Finally, Colonel Drake stood up and moved to the front of the group.

"Frankly, I would be inclined to believe this lovely lady if it weren't for the fact that she was not witness to the acts of provocation that occurred at the northern boundary of the reservation. In the heat of battle, she may have also misunderstood the actions of the soldiers she accuses of attacking her. According to Private Weston, he and two others were trying to take her away from the camp in order to protect her. They were concerned that she might become a victim of the Indian blood lust that was running amok at the time. The unfortunate confusion, smoke, noise and chaos of the situation led to total misunderstanding of the actions of my men and unfortunately Mr. Cadwallader irresponsibly attacked them and murdered two in cold blood."

Amanda listened and when he finished, she said simply:

"That is not true."

The group, assuaged by the plausible and preferred explanation offered by Colonel Drake, resumed a noisy exchange of opinions, ending as with most group think conclusions that the preferred view far outweighed the disappointing evidence of facts and truth. The Mayor called for order and suggested the community send another message to authorities back east requesting additional military protection against further Indian onslaughts and some punitive measures, including removing the Sioux to an area more remote from white settlement. This measure was approved by acclamation and the group then broke up for refreshments and further exchanges of opinion and speculation designed mainly to solidify a consensus sufficient to make further pursuit of the truth unnecessary.

Within a week the Attorney General in Washington sent an order for the arrest of Philip Cadwallader on charges of murder and conspiracy to arm Indian tribes contrary to treaty and Federal law. He was to be returned to Ablilene, Kansas, for detention and trial. Enforcement of the order belonged to the local civil authorities and fell finally on Sheriff Westmoreland. The Sheriff was in his office when the order was delivered to him. He had offered his room to Philip as a refuge, but town sentiment was now so against the Indians and Philip that it seemed more unsafe than otherwise. He told Philip to camp out in a cottonwood grove along the river and he would keep him abreast of developments. He would protect him from any action on the civil side, but couldn't vouch for Colonel Drake and the military. So far as they were concerned, Philip was fair game and the sooner he was brought in, dead or alive, the better. He and Amanda were the last witnesses against them.

Philip rode out to the grove where he and Amanda had picnicked. There were many cottonwoods that provided sufficient cover to conceal him, at least for a time. He met with the Chiefs several days before the order was received. They had not decided what to do but were organizing their defense and arming as best they could. Half of the braves had rifles and had added to their reserve what they had captured from the attacking soldiers. But they had limited ammunition and were concerned about what the military might be ordered to do next. They were prepared to fight to the last rather than be disarmed and be herded off like cattle. They were militant and angry and prepared for the worst. Philip could offer little to reassure them but the remote prospect of intervention on their behalf of the Indian Bureau and sympathizers in Congress. They politely listened and disbelieved.

Two days later, Grey Fox from Canada arrived. The Chiefs consulted with him and decided to move north on their own. They would fight defensive actions on the way if necessary, but they would not provoke hostilities. They notified Philip and urged him to join them. His position was hopeless. Accused of murder and conspiracy, facing a white jury in Abilene with a lone woman to defend him and the organized prevarication of Fort Polk against him, he would certainly be convicted and hanged. That is, if he got to Abiline alive. Too many interests would prefer to see him dead and buried, let the incident be forgotten, and the march of progress resume without him or the Indians. Philip found the arguments hard to disagree with.

The party at the Double-B ranch, shaken by the death of Ariadne and the Indian matter, was divided on everything but the need to return east as soon as possible and leave the horror behind. Amanda wanted to defend Philip should he go to trial. She wanted to fight for justice for the Indians. Braddock, uncomfortable in his double role, wanted to leave. Sir Charles was more than ready. Lord Basil insisted, and Raymond was desperate. The departure was mutually agreed for the following Sunday, four days away. Amanda was desperate to see Philip. She rode to town on Friday morning and spoke to Sheriff Westmoreland. He told her where Philip was camping out. She rode there directly. A steady wind blew from the north, bowing the grass, moving formations of clouds and migrating birds high above the Great Plains. The sun began its final descent against the saw blade of the Rocky Mountains just showing a darker shade of cobalt blue at the limit of the horizon. She dismounted and went into the grove. She saw the waving sea of prairie grass, listened to the rushing sound like a surf rising and falling in the warm wind. He ran to meet her. They looked at each other for a moment and then he took her in his arms. They found it difficult to say anything, to find words to begin. Philip looked into the distance, then to the ground.

"Too much is stacked against me Amanda. I have to leave."

The words stabbed deep into his heart, choked his chest and throat. He turned away to hide the tears burning in his eyes.

"I love you Amanda, but I don't know how it would ever work out. It would take a paradise and we don't live in paradise."

She looked at him. She felt the love and the hopelessness between them. Their strange, wonderful attraction across the ruin of their beautiful beginning. How did it happen that she should love this man from another world, and he should love her? And where in the world could they possibly find a place for the wonder of what they felt for each other? How could such feeling survive, how could it not? He turned, walked over to her, kissed her on the forehead as she turned her face up at him.

"Good bye Amanda. God bless you. God bless you."

He could barely choke out the words. Tears streamed down her face as she stood looking up at him, smiling. He took her hands and kissed them, then slowly returned them to her side. He turned, walked over to his horse, and mounted. Facing her once more, for a long, long moment, they looked at each other. He turned his horse and slowly rode off, outlined against the sunset, as she stood there watching him, joy, love, pain, filling her heart, the sweet earth smells and the freshening wind lifting her hair, the sky streaked with thin clouds sweeping from horizon to horizon, the prairie murmur humming to her, as she saw him slowly move farther and farther through the endless grassland toward the beckoning mountains beyond.

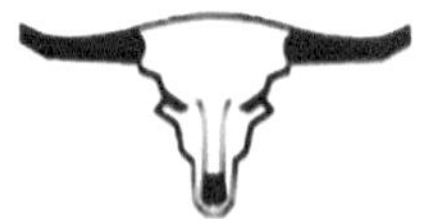

Westmoreland sent a note to Colonel Drake: *'It's time. Meet me at the Post Office tomorrow at noon.'* Drake usually went to the Post Office on Thursday. Westmoreland knew that. Drake decided to go as usual. He had been feeling unwell. The morphine did not work as effectively as in the past. Sometimes he felt a tremor run through his body. He increased the dose, which helped, but a shaking in his right hand made it necessary to abruptly end knife and firing practice.

Westmoreland opened the trunk which had remained closed for most of the seventeen years since the Civil War ended. The faded and raveled grey tunic with the gold-thread braiding and gold-plated stars on the high collar looked much as they had then, giving off a faint odor of gun powder, smoke, musty wool. He unfolded the coat, undid the buttons with the letters CSA in gold plate, worn to the underlying brass in spots. He put his arm through the sleeve. A thrill moved through his body. The tunic fit as it had when he first wore it to a formal ball in 1862. Lenore sewed it for him, stood proudly by him as President and Mrs. Davis welcomed them to Atlanta. He buttoned the buttons and stood at attention in front of the dresser mirror. The faded sepia photograph of Lenore and Melissa, then five years old, was in the original silver frame. She smiled the loving, brave smile of the concealed hopelessness of a soldier's wife trying to show no sign of concern that might undermine her husband's ordeal of duty. He saw through her bravery and loved her even more.

He took up his Confederate gun belt and put it on. He picked up the Confederate Army cavalry officer's broad-brimmed hat with gold braid and put it on. His eyes welled with tears as he stood looking into the mirror, hearing the bugles, the war cry of his men advancing on the Union forces, the deafening sound of shot and cannon, the bitter smoke and dust, the screams of wounded men and horses and mules, the senseless delirium of battle moving as if in a nightmare until somehow the noise abates and you find through no fault or merit of your own you are on the winning or losing side, and it seems in the end not to matter which it is. He saluted the uniform in the mirror, then felt foolish, then felt proud and saluted again for all the men and women of the Old South who bore the burden of hopeless victory and inevitable defeat through five years of war and misery, showing no sign of fear, no disposition to surrender, no glimmer of defeatism or despair, smiling and gracious to the end.

He turned toward the door, left it open, and headed down the hall to the stairs. The noonday light shone sharply through the front door of the hotel. He stepped onto the porch and headed down the steps to the street. The first passersby did double takes as they saw the familiar Sheriff in the surprising Confederate uniform. Word spread fast as clerks and customers came out of stores to look. Women rushed their children past him as he walked slowly down the dead center of main street heading for the Post Office. Colonel Drake regularly came to town Thursdays with mail pouches to be delivered to Abiline. That he might not come today never crossed Westmoreland's mind. He kept walking slowly forward to the Post Office. The street was now deserted, although the verandas, porches and boardwalks in front of stores, saloon, and bank were crowded with men, women and children, quietly murmuring, sensing something strange, possibly momentous, frightening, inevitable like the clash of natural forces that cannot be prevented, obstructed or deferred.

At the end of the street a figure in dress blue uniform stepped off the veranda of the Post Office. Colonel Drake was sweating. He had taken morphine an hour before, but it had not calmed him down. He was in full dress uniform and wore the cavalry officer's Colt 45 in his holster. He carried a Bowie knife in his boot. He wore pale yellow doeskin gloves. His eyes were red from whisky and morphine, but this did not show under the smart blue wide brimmed hat with the gold braid. He looked good and held himself impressively.

They approached each other one-hundred yards apart: slowly, unhurried, graceful, careful, wary. Westmoreland looked steadily at Drake, waiting for the first time he could be sure they saw eye to eye. All malice had seeped away. He was in a ritual with no personal content, merely the instrument of justice, not revenge or honor or whatever large purpose men killed themselves for. Lenore and Melissa were there in spirit, were the reason for his being there. But he and they knew that nothing would bring them back, and Drake had paid already in a different kind of Hell for his crimes. Yet they had to face off and end the cycle of violence once and for ever.

Drake removed his gloves, first the right then the left. He tucked them in his belt not losing stride. He touched the butt of his revolver with the heel of his hand in a slow motion, showing Westmoreland he was not making any move in particular, just to gauge the position of the Colt. He felt tired suddenly, and his hand began to shake barely perceptibly. The morphine was not working.

They were fifty yards apart. Westmoreland could see Drake's eyes. He fixed them and advanced a bit more slowly. Drake's right hand began to shake enough that Westmoreland could detect it. Drake tried desperately to control any sign of the trembling. They were now thirty yards apart, easily within deadly range, impossible to miss. Westmoreland continued forward. Drake stopped, legs apart. He felt queasy, pain was working through his body. He wanted to reach for the whisky flask in his tunic but was held back by some trace of dignity, some sense that people were watching an officer of the United States Army, something of the West Point code, something long lost or forgotten in the Hell of war and the greater Hell of morphine addiction.

Drake stood straight as Westmoreland continued to walk forward. They were now twenty yards apart. Drake moved for his revolver. Westmorland, through the split-second assessment only the experienced fighter can make, realized that Drake was disabled in some way that made it impossible for him to carry out the action he had started. Instead of reaching for his gun, Westmoreland continued walking forward. Drake tried to grip the butt of the Colt, managed to pull it out of his holster. His hand shook as he tried to raise it. He couldn't make his hand move upward. He grasped his right wrist with his left hand. The barrel rose slightly. He tried to pull the trigger. Westmoreland was ten yards away. Drake's fingers wouldn't move, his hand was trembling, and he couldn't keep the Colt level or steady. Westmoreland looked into Drake's eyes. Drake looked back, his face dripping with sweat, his eye twitching, his jaw set. His shoulders were shaking and now his knees began to buckle. His hand shook violently as he dropped to one knee. He fired into the ground, tried to lift the Colt, failed, and fired into the ground again. He tried to stand up, but his knee wouldn't lock fast. He couldn't get enough strength to lift himself.

Westmoreland stood in front of Drake and reached for the Colt. It fell from Drake's hand. Westmoreland picked up the Colt, emptied the chamber of all but one unfired bullet, and handed it back to Drake. He then turned and walked back to the hotel, slowly, not proud, not happy, not satisfied, disgusted with the blight of war and violence, the notion that any man's dishonor could ever be a source of satisfaction and not of shame, as tears stung his eyes. Drake continued the struggle to raise himself, lift himself from the dust of main street, from physical ruin, from the abyss of pain that engulfed him eighteen years before. Westmoreland reached the front of the jail when he heard the shot. He stopped, turned slowly, came to attention, saluted the still blue form lying forty yards away, turned again and continued to the hotel. That night he took his Confederate uniform behind the hotel and burned it. The next day he packed and took the train west to California. For Westmoreland, the Civil War was finally over.

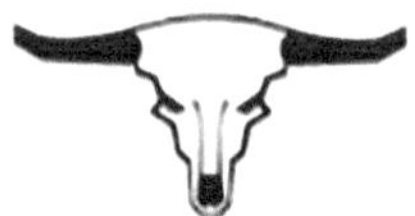

The party at Double-B ranch planned to leave on Sunday by the morning train. All were packed and ready by Saturday. Over the past week they had their meals separately, given the turmoil and divisions, the confusion and violence that made company difficult to bear.

Sir Charles visited Ariadne's grave on Saturday morning. It was marked by a wooden cross on a windswept hill that served as graveyard for Del Norte. He stood over the grave for an hour, then rode back to the ranch and returned to his room. Until now he had not realized how deep his feelings for her were. He thought of Alice, her mother, how he had never taken time to grow close to her, so preoccupied with his career and ambition. He sat on the bed, looking at photographs of Ariadne and Alice, which he had left for last to pack. From somewhere in the depth of his soul a tidal wave of remorse rose up, as he suddenly burst into uncontrollable sobbing.

"Ariadne, Ariadne, Ariadne…"

He wept for several minutes. Some long-denied part of himself, made accessible by fatigue, moral exhaustion, despair, emerged, breaking down all his habits of thought and feeling. He stared inwardly for many minutes, as the shift in values, feelings, understanding occurred. He would never be the same again. He walked over to the desk and took up pen and paper. He began to write, slowly at first, then with a kind of urgent desperation as though the sooner and more completely he could tell the truth the more likely a just conclusion to the terrible events of their trip would occur. He wrote at the top of the page:

A true account of the recent assault on the Sioux Indian reservation

by Sir Charles Winthrop

He wrote for nearly two hours. When he concluded he felt a kind of peace. He folded the pages and packed them in his valise, resolved that when he reached New York he would release them to the newspapers, in partial expiation of the long violence he had done to his wife, to his daughter, to others, to himself.

Braddock had the latest mining reports which proved to be ambiguous as to the return the mines were likely to yield. He was already thinking of how best to keep the venture alive, and how to deal with the evident and growing disinterest of Sir Charles and Lord Basil in the project. Lord Basil and Raymond celebrated the departure with dinner and champagne in Basil's now shared suite. They exchanged highly amusing observations of the American West and delighted prospects for return to Oxford. The morning would bring new directions and different destinies to each member of the party.

Amanda had resolved to visit Philip's parents and attempt, with them, to exonerate him and promote an investigation into the attack on the Indians and the false charges against Philip. The night before departure she stayed in her room until nearly sunset then decided to walk over the hill behind the house to see one last time the long serpentine path of the river visible for many miles from the high ground. A soft breeze rose from the cluster of cottonwoods that began at the foot of the hill and ran up the drainage halfway to the top. Summer prairie grass, renourished by the early morning rain, blanketed the gentle curve of the hill, here and there tipped with madder and violet from the flame of the setting sun behind its distant edge. The odd-angled stakes of a fence filed down toward the trees, the bleached grey oak catching fire from a few red-bottomed clouds overhead. Amanda unlatched the fence gate and walked westward. The sky, already turning indigo behind the house, formed a dome of dark ultramarine, turning brighter and cerulean as it fell like a waterfall into the molten reds and yellows of the sunset.

She walked, slowly swinging her bonnet against the scattered wildflowers and tall grass, following the path, always overgrown in summer, that led to the top of the hill. In weeks past she would turn toward the trees, finding the small clearing where she had read and dreamed away summer afternoons. A clutch of waxwings flew overhead looping and diving, then flying off toward the trees, as a mockingbird perched on a fence stake threw a melodic line over the accompanying livestock murmurs, strumming insects, and bird chatter. Smells of grass and earth and tree bark spread through the evening air as she absorbed the warmth, the smells, the sounds, the play of colors. For a moment she stopped, closed her eyes, and lifted her face toward the sky, the amber light warming her body like candles. She resumed walking, the trees to her left darkly etched along the lower part of the hill. *There will be time…. there will be time.*

From the fence line you could see her outlined in the sunset, her light dress glowing against the dark velvet grass. The sun had nearly set, leaving a molten sliver of orange-red receding at the edge of night. Amanda continued to walk toward the top of the hill as above and behind her a shower of stars winked in the darkening sky, choiring their song of hope through the breeze-lifted strands of her radiant hair.

FINISH